Legacy of Evil

Marshal Jason Brand decides he is due a break after his last assignment, so he rides off to Mexico – in the company of a young woman named Sarita. But his peace is soon shattered by the old Apache, Nante, who asks Brand to bring in those of his people who have been enticed away to the Sierra Madre badlands by the renegade, Benito.

And so it is that Brand saddles up and sets off on the dangerous trail after Benito. The way is treacherous and Brand has to use all his skill and his guns to reach the Sierra Madre.

Then when he finally arrives, there are surprises in store as he must face old enemies. Can he, will he, live long enough to fulfil his promise to Nante?

A Jason Brand Novel

Legacy of Evil

NEIL HUNTER

A Black Horse Western

ROBERT HALE · LONDON

© Neil Hunter 2004
First published in Great Britain 2004

ISBN 0 7090 7506 5

Robert Hale Limited
Clerkenwell House
Clerkenwell Green
London EC1R 0HT

Typeset by
Derek Doyle & Associates, Liverpool.
Printed and bound in Great Britain by
Antony Rowe Limited, Wiltshire

CHAPTER 1

Jason Brand stretched out a lazy hand and picked up the bottle of *pulque*. Raising it against the bright sunlight he saw it was almost empty. He put the bottle to his lips and drank, draining the last of the liquid. His thirst satisfied for the time being he turned the bottle upside down and watched the few remaining drops drip from the neck. The moment they hit the dry, dusty ground the drops were instantly absorbed. Brand sighed. The sound of a contented man. For the first time in years he could honestly admit to being totally satisfied with his lot. He leaned his broad shoulders against the sun-warmed adobe wall of the tiny hut. It was hot and quiet. So quiet he could hear the trickle of water in the narrow creek below the hut. Forcing himself to move he raised his head and watched the kneeling figure of the young Mexican woman washing clothes in the clear stream. Just seeing her there raised a warm stirring in his loins. In his fertile mind he could visualize the brown sleekness of her strong, lithe body. Full breasts and firm, supple thighs.

On more than one occasion he admitted his luck had been in when he had gone looking for the girl called Sarita. It had been more than three months now since he had ridden away from that little town in Louisiana, leaving behind the memory of a beautiful young woman named Sarah and the silent cemetery where she lay. He hadn't even been sure where he was heading, just as long as it took him away from that place. He had drifted, letting his instincts take him back to familiar territory. Days later, in a more rational frame of mind, he had turned up in that nameless town where he had once met a girl named Sarita.

It seemed a lifetime ago. He'd been working for a man named Dorsey, trying to find the man's kidnapped daughter, and Sarita had been a diversion along the way. She had asked him to come back to her, and though he had said he would, his world had become so hectic and involved that his promise had drifted into his memory. When he had asked for her he had been told that she had gone back to Sonora to look after her aged grandfather, somewhere below Agua Prieta. The old man had a run-down farm and he was getting too old to run it any longer. Sarita was his only living relative, so she had quit her job in the cantina and left for Sonora.

Brand had hung around the town for a few days, then on an impulse he had taken the trail for Sonora. A week later, filthy and unshaven, he had ridden across the narrow creek and reined in before the tiny adobe. It wasn't much of a farm. A few chickens. A couple of rutting pigs in a derelict pen.

Nearby was a tethered goat. The animal had broken off from chewing at the grass to stare at him. Brand had noticed something else. Across from the hut, on the far side of the dusty yard, was a fresh grave with a crude wooden marker.

He had caught a glimpse of movement inside the hut. Then she had stepped outside, a hand raised across her eyes to block out the bright sunlight as she stared up at him. Brand realized she didn't recognize him. Not surprising. He'd lost some weight and he was filthy and unshaven.

'Hello, Sarita,' he had greeted as he climbed down off his horse.

She'd come closer, peering at him, seeking the man beneath the whiskers and the layers of dirt, and then her face had brightened and she had thrown herself at him.

'Brand? Is it you, *hombre*?' She had scanned his face intently. 'It is you! I knew some day you would come back to me.'

She had kissed him. Fussed over him. Made him a meal and prepared him a hot bath. And that had been that.

From that moment they had settled into a comfortable existence. The pace of life was slow and undemanding. There wasn't a deal to do around the tiny farm. The grave Brand had seen was where Sarita's grandfather lay buried. He had died only a week before Brand's arrival, leaving Sarita alone, and for her own reasons she had decided to stay on and run the place herself. She had little reason to return to her former life. It had been pointless, with not much promise. Here on the farm she had at least some peace, and a little dignity in the work she did.

And then like a miracle Jason Brand had ridden back into her life. For the first few days she never took her eyes off him, trying to convince herself that it was true. That he was really there and was not a dream. She watched him. Touched him. Secretly smiled to herself. He was back with her and she was happy. She had truly been blessed.

Despite all these things there was a nagging doubt at the back of her mind. A doubt as to how permanent their situation was. He seemed content enough now. But how long would he remain so? She watched the brooding grimness ease from his face. Saw his eyes take on a new brightness. He had told her about the woman who had died, and Sarita could sense how he had felt about her. Sarita was not jealous. Only sad for the loss of the woman. She knew he was a man who needed his women like some men need drink. He was relaxed now, looking no further than the creek running beside the farm. But one day he would raise his gaze beyond that narrow boundary, seeing the jagged rise of the distant hills, and his longing for the wider world would return. She knew this in her heart. It saddened her because she knew she would not be able to do anything to stop him when that time came. All she could do was be happy with him now.

Those thoughts were in Sarita's mind as she finished folding the clothing she had just washed. She picked it up and turned away from the creek, walking back towards the hut. The hard ground was warm beneath her bare feet and she felt the sun burn pleasantly through her blouse. She could see Brand stretched out, his back against the wall of the adobe. As she neared him he raised the empty bottle.

'It's empty, woman,' he said gently.

Santa brushed stray hair away from her face and smiled down at him.

'Then perhaps you will have to go thirsty,' she said and walked on by into the hut. She put down the clothing and reached for the last bottle on the shelf. She took it outside. Found he had gone from where she had left him. Glancing around she saw him by the rickety fence of the corral that held his horse and the farm's pair of mules.

'Hey, *hombre*,' she called.

Brand turned as she brought him the bottle. He watched her pull out the stopper.

'You want this?' she asked, leaning her supple body against his.

He took the bottle from her and drank. He felt a warm glow build in his stomach. He couldn't be certain what was causing it. The drink – or the inviting softness of her thrusting body.

'Brand, it is very hot.' Her voice was low and honey-sweet. 'Inside it is shady and on the bed are cool sheets.'

Brand lowered the bottle.

'I have just realized you only want me for my body.'

Sarita smiled, eyes bright with anticipation. '*Si!* But is it not a good reason?'

'Best I've heard today, ma'am.'

They turned back for the hut, and that was when

Brand saw the two riders splashing across the creek. One was white, riding a slow mule. The other, lean and wiry, was an Apache. Young in years, but with a wisdom beyond his age showing in his glittering eyes. They were coming on slowly. Men not in any kind of a hurry, but men who knew exactly where they were heading.

Brand felt the girl stiffen, fingers digging into his arm.

'Easy,' he said. 'They're friendly.'

'You know them?'

'One of them.'

The pair of riders drew rein, one slightly behind the other, leaving Brand to confront an old acquaintance.

They faced each other for a time, recalling events that had left scars on them both. Incidents that still left their marks.

'You a hard feller to find, Jason.'

Brand smiled and held out a hand. The fingers that closed over his were still strong. Still able to match his own powerful grasp.

'Maybe because I didn't want to be found, Al. That why they sent you? Nobody hides from you for long.'

Al Sieber, Army Chief of Apache Scouts, working out of the San Carlos Indian Agency, eased his stocky body out of the saddle and stamped the stiffness from his joints. Brand hadn't seen the German-born scout for a long time, yet from what he saw now Sieber hadn't changed at all. The rounded, mustachioed face, brown as old saddle leather, bore the same bluff, good-natured expression as it always had.

Sieber showed a pleasant personality that hid an inner toughness to match any. When Sieber was friendly it was fine. But when he was in a violent mood it was wise to stay well clear.

Watching his old friend now Brand became aware of one thing – if Al Sieber had trailed him all the way down here to Sonora it hadn't been for the ride. Sieber wanted him for something and it wasn't to ask him the time of day.

'Sarita, would you make us some coffee, please,' Brand asked.

The Mexican girl stared at him for a long moment, knowing deep inside that her fears were about to come true. The day she had been dreading had arrived. Brand would soon be leaving her. This man who had come looking for him would offer something Brand would be unable to refuse. It would be a call back to his old life. As day followed night it was certain Brand would go. He was a *pistolero*, a man of the gun, and it was the one thing he could never resist. The violence and the challenge was in his blood, and Jason Brand could no more turn his back on it than he could stop breathing. She had accepted this from the day he had arrived. They had both known it would have to end eventually. Brand would ride on and she would be alone again.

'*Sí*, I will make the coffee,' she said and went into the hut.

'Pretty little thing,' Sieber said with genuine regret in his voice. 'She's going to miss you.'

'Careful, Al, you came close to apologizing,' Brand said. 'Anyhow, what makes you think I'm leaving?'

11

Sieber was gazing around as if he hadn't heard.

'Nice place you got here.'

'Ain't mine, Al. It belongs to the girl, and I asked you a question.'

'Like I said. Nice place. For an old man to retire to.'

'Horse shit isn't your style, Al. You didn't ride all the way from San Carlos to admire the scenery. And I ain't about to sit out my days watching the sunsets.'

Brand handed over the bottle and watched Sieber take a long swallow.

'By damn, that's a pretty good brew.' Sieber wiped his lips and turned to his riding companion, who still sat his horse, watching silently. 'Hey, Kid, take the animals to drink. I reckon we stay the night.'

For the first time Brand took a good look at Sieber's Apache companion. He looked to be around seventeen to eighteen years old, darkly good looking. He wore a dark-blue Army shirt with the stripes of a sergeant on the sleeve. At first glance he was just another Apache, one of the bucks who scouted for Al Sieber. But when Brand took a deeper look he saw there was more to this one. The Apache caught Brand's gaze and held it. Staring into those dark bright eyes, Brand knew he was looking at an unusual Apache. What he didn't know that day, nor did Al Sieber, was that they were in the presence of a young Apache destined to become a living legend. Within a year the Apache Kid – as he would become known throughout the South-west – embarked on his lone war against the Army, leading them across the vast territory as they vainly tried to capture him.

Sometimes they came close, but during the eight years that was the span of the Kid's epic battle against the US Cavalry, he was always one step ahead. He killed and destroyed as and when he wanted. Feared and respected he finally vanished. The legend had it that he died in some lonely mountain place. Others swore he'd gone over the border into the wilderness of the Mexican badlands. In time legend and fact became one, the edges blurred by the telling and retelling. The Apache Kid did vanish, and only one man knew the truth of the way it ended. But not on that hot day as the Kid turned his gaze away and led his pony and Sieber's mule down to the creek. The story's end was something for the future – it still had to have its beginnings.

Brand returned to his spot against the adobe wall and sat down. He waited for Sieber to join him. The scout dropped to his heels in front of Brand and took another swallow from the bottle.

'Old friend wants to see you pretty bad,' Sieber said.

'Yeah?'

For the first time in weeks Brand thought about McCord, and the remembering conjured a picture of a quiet little cemetery in Louisiana. He reached out to snatch the bottle from Sieber and drank deeply.

'Hit a raw nerve, did I, *schichobe*?' Sieber failed to get a response and didn't probe any deeper. Brand's private thoughts were his own, and Sieber respected that in a man. So he let the moment pass, waiting until the hard look drifted from Brand's eyes. 'Nante's back at San Carlos. Hurt bad and dyin'. But swears he won't let *Yussen* take him until he speaks to you.'

This time Brand's eyes settled on the scout's face. The interest was showing now.

Nante!

Brand had clashed with the old Apache many times over the years. The last time they had met had been during Brand's pursuit of the half-breed Lobo. Nante had been taking his people into Mexico, trying to give them a chance to gather strength and rest before they continued their futile war against the Army. Brand had wondered whether he would ever see the old warrior again.

It seemed he might. But what did Nante consider so important in his time before death?

'What's it all about, Al?'

Sieber shrugged his wide shoulders.

'The old feller won't say. He just keep on asking for you.'

'He bring his people in with him?'

Sieber shook his head.

'Came in with no more than three. They had their hands full keepin' Nante alive. He was in a hell of a state. Cut to rags and carrying a few chunks of lead.'

'Any ideas?'

'Way I figure maybe one of the young bucks took over and booted the old man out. Been a lot of pretty bad raids along the border of late. Worse than usual. An' I hear tell 'bout some white god come to lead the 'Pache to victory over the Army. Kind of talk that pulls in every bronco in the territory. Even got the Carlos Indians restless. Things are hotting up. Crook

14

is getting close to sweet talkin' Geronimo into surrender. Most other Apache bigwigs are watching and listening. Geronimo comes in we figure so will others . . .'

Sieber slammed a big fist against the ground. 'If this bunch who threw Nante out keep on raiding the peace talks are going to blow to hell. Hell, Jason, you know how these things go out here. Only takes one bad incident to spoil it all. Cannot happen. This time I got a feeling the talks could stop all the killing.'

'Anything in this white god talk?'

Sieber shrugged.

'You always hear this kind of nonsense. Some big muckey-muck out of the clouds leading the way to victory. Maybe some crazy buck got hisself smoked up on peyote and saw himself a vision. Jesus, you know how they are. Most likely it's all big wind.' Sieber dragged off his hat, scratching at his head. 'Could be some white renegade stirring 'em up. Feeding 'em whiskey and trading guns.'

'Wouldn't be the first time.'

'Jason, I figure Nante knows what's going on. But ain't about to tell anyone 'cept you, so come morning we saddle up and ride.'

Brand stared over Sieber's shoulder, watching the young Apache making camp beside the creek. Pale fingers of smoke rose into the sky from a small fire he'd already started. The smoke rose in a straight line. Not a breath of wind to disturb it. He realized he was going to miss this place. He had been getting into a routine. Too much of a routine. Thinking on he realized that Sieber had showed up just in time.

Sarita came outside with tin mugs and a pot of coffee. She handed the mugs to Brand and Sieber and filled them. She indicated the Apache squatting by the creek.

'Shall I take him some?'

Sieber shook his head.

'He sees to his own needs. No need to worry about the Kid.'

His words would soon come back to haunt him.

Brand caught Sarita's eye.

'In the morning I have to go,' he said simply.

Sarita regarded him silently. A faint, wistful smile curved her lips before she murmured: '*Sí.*' She said no more as she turned and went back inside the hut.

'Nice coffee,' Sieber offered in the silence that followed. There was no reply so he buried his face in his mug and carried on drinking.

Down at the creek the young Apache sat and watched the clear flowing water. Though his face was turned toward the creek his eyes were seeing far distant horizons beyond high, solitary mountains that existed only in his mind. He dreamed dreams that had no meaning even to him at that time. He dwelled on events that had yet to take place. In his mind he saw the death of the Apache nation. The destruction of *The People*, and he was torn between the loyalty he had for his tribe and that which he had for the blue shirt he wore with its yellow stripes on the sleeve. He carried pride in his heart for the man named Sieber, the chief of scouts he served so faithfully. His confusion grew stronger the longer he pondered.

Which way to go? The right path to walk?

It was only recently that the dreams had come to haunt him, though he knew that some day soon he would have to make his stand for one or the other. When that time came it would not be of his own choosing, though once again he was not aware of that yet. His path would be chosen for him, decided by tragic events, and once he took his first steps along that destined way there would be no going back. His stand would make him known throughout the land.

He would become a legend.

An outlaw.

And the end was already written.

CHAPTER 2

Over the main administration building the weath-ered sign said it all:

SAN CARLOS INDIAN AGENCY
ARIZONA TERRITORY.

A ragtag collection of adobe buildings, a few tents, and the usual scattering of litter denoted the pres-ence of the human animal. The place looked no different from the last time Jason Brand had been there, and that had been a few years back. Some of the brown, impassive faces that stared up at him as he rode by looked the same; a little older and wiser in their knowledge of the *Pinda Lickoyi* and his promises. As always those lined, stoic faces gave noth-ing away.

It was breathlessly hot. Dust hung in the still air. Somewhere a dog barked; a thin, agitated sound that quickly faded in the vastness of the wide land. Brand didn't like San Carlos. There was a feeling of being closed in. There were no fences. No barbed-wire, but the place still had the atmosphere of a prison. The Apaches could move about with relative freedom, yet every one of the Indians considered himself a prisoner – if not in body then surely of the soul.

'You still not like this place?' Sieber asked as they rode in.

They had debated the San Carlos policy many times, and never agreed.

'Damn right there,' Brand grumbled sourly.

They dismounted outside the main building. Tied their horses to a rail that was cracked and warped from the heat. Brand straightened his aching back, rubbing at his spine. It had been a long ride up from Mexico. Sieber had been sparing in his rest periods. It had proved one thing to Brand. He *had* been getting lazy. His life with Sarita had been good, but the lazy days had been softening him up. The San Carlos trip had certainly worked out the excesses of food and drink. Not that he regretted any of it.

Sieber's young Apache vanished silently, leaving Brand and Sieber to go about their own business.

'Nante's hut is over there,' Sieber said, leading the way.

Brand followed. He glanced around the agency, eventually coming out with the question that had been on his lips since they had sighted the place.

'Tom Horn still riding for you?'

Sieber glanced across at him, a smile edging his lips.

'What the hell between you two? Always sparring, I recall. Never tell me what troubled you.'

'Never took to him, Al. Something about him.

Can't put my finger on. I just know he's a mean son of a bitch, and one day it'll show.'

'I remember same kind of things said about you, Jason. You figure they right?'

It was Brand's turn to smile.

'Hell, Al, we're both just a pair of mean bone-heads.'

'Now you talk some kind of sense. Good to meet a man who can look in a mirror and see himself as he is.'

They reached the hut Sieber had indicated. It was small and shabby. The thin door hung open on sagging rawhide hinges. A clay water *olla* sat just outside the door. As Sieber and Brand reached the hut a dark-haired Apache girl stepped through the door and bent to pick up the *olla*. As she straightened she saw them, nodding briefly in Sieber's direction. Then she glanced at Brand, assessing him quickly. She was young, he saw. Nineteen – maybe twenty at most. Pretty too, with large oval eyes in a strong-boned face. Her mouth was a little wide maybe, but it did nothing to detract from her natural beauty. She wore a simple buckskin dress that molded itself to her supple, full-breasted body. She had a flat belly and rounded hips that flowed into strong thighs. Her black hair, held from her face by a soft band, hung in a gleaming fall that went below her shoulders.

'Nante still lives,' the girl said. She was still looking at Brand. 'Is this the one he asks for?'

'Jason Brand,' Sieber said.

'Nante's faith in you has kept him alive,' the girl

said. 'But I see only a man. Are you different from the other *Pinda Lickoyi?*'

'If Nante believes it it is good enough for me,' Sieber said.

The girl stared at Brand a moment longer, then rested the *olla* on her hip and walked away.

'Nante's granddaughter. Her mother died in childbirth. Father killed at Geronimo's side. She is called Niana.'

They went inside the hut, bending as they stepped through the low doorway. Dust motes floated in the bright shafts of sunlight filtering in through gaps in the roof. The interior was bare, save for a small charcoal fire that glowed from a cut-down oil drum. Perched on top of the fire was a battered, blackened coffee pot that Brand recognized. It raised a brief smile.

'I offer coffee to you, Brand.'

The voice came from the far side of the hut. A thin figure lay beneath a blanket, a wrinkled brown face watching intently. Brand crouched beside the withered form, shocked at what he saw. Nante had aged beyond his years. He was old, Brand knew. When they had met before the Apache warrior had carried his years with pride. As Nante raised himself to a sitting position and the blanket slipped away, he exposed a broken and ravaged body. His flesh was torn and seared by terrible wounds.

'You should have been here the day he came in,' Sieber said. 'On foot he was. Trailing blood with every step. Someone treat him bad.'

Brand caught the Apache's gaze.

'Who did this, Nante?'

The old Apache looked beyond Brand to where Sieber stood. His dark eyes glittered with undiminished pride. After a moment Sieber raised a big hand in surrender.

'I go.'

When they were alone Nante touched Brand's arm and indicated the coffee pot. Brand found a couple of tin mugs next to the fire. He poured hot, black coffee and returned to where Nante had propped himself against the wall of the hut, the blanket draped across his thin body. He took the mug Brand offered with a thin hand covered in near-transparent skin.

'Anything you need to say you could have told Sieber,' Brand said. 'He's a good man, Nante. You know that. So why me?'

The old warrior watched as Brand squatted on the dirt floor beside him.

'You kept your promise and killed the crazy one called Lobo,' Nante said. There was a distant look in his eyes. 'I wish I had seen it.'

'He damn near killed me,' Brand replied. He took a sip of the coffee. It was strong and it burnt – the way Nante liked it. 'Still doesn't answer my question. Why send Sieber to find me?'

Nante's shoulders stiffened under the blanket.

'We are dying, Brand. The Apache is dying. Our time is short and we cannot fight the Army any longer. If there is not an end to the war the Apache will be no more. Sieber has talked to Mangas and Geronimo. Soon there will be talk of peace. Maybe this time it will come.' Nante paused. The effort of talking was taking its toll. 'Brand, I wanted my people to surrender. I saw the young men dying but we were not winning the fight. It saddened me. I wished a better life for them but they did not heed my words. I told them it was foolish to carry on. But the warriors had found a new leader. A younger man with the fire of war in his blood. He is called Benito. His words were listened to and the warriors believed.'

Nante reached out to grip Brand's arm. 'Then Benito brought the *Pinda Lickoyi*. A white who showed my people new guns and ammunition. A wagon filled with these things. There was whiskey and food for the little ones. My people believed Benito had brought a new spirit. But I saw evil in the eye of the *Pinda Lickoyi*. He brought them because *he* wanted the whites dead as much as the Apache.

'He hates his own kind, Brand. I saw this and tried to show my people, but Benito turned them against me. For two days they put me to the torture. They would have killed me if I had not escaped. When my pony died I walked to San Carlos to find Sieber. I knew he would find you and bring you to me before I died.'

Nante slumped back against the wall, the mug of coffee in his drooping fingers. A thin trickle of blood slid from the corner of his mouth. The old warrior had been hurt more than Brand realized, and it angered him to see it.

'What can I do, Nante?'

'Go to Mexico. Find my people and bring them home. Away from Benito and his warpath. My heart saddens to think of them here at San Carlos. But even here is better than the life they would have under Benito and his *Pinda Lickoyi*. Sieber talks of peace, and I believe him. Yet how can there be a true peace if Benito stays on the blood trail? Who will believe the Apache promises while there is still killing? Is this not true, Brand?'

Brand nodded. He saw the logic in Nante's argument. It wasn't going to make any peace talks plausible while there were still Apaches on the rampage.

'Nante, I don't even know where your people are. Mexico is one hell of a piece of territory.'

'There is a place in Sonora. High in the Sierra Madre. It is a place I have used many times. No one has ever found it. Not even the *Rurales* or the *Yaqui* trackers.'

'Doesn't make it easy for me then.'

'There is one more who knows the trail,' Nante whispered, his voice starting to fade.

'Who?' Brand asked.

'I know the trail.'

Brand had not heard anyone enter the hut. He turned to see the young Apache girl, Niana, standing behind him. Over his shoulder she saw Nante; concern clouded her eyes. She moved to him, speaking in rapid Apache. His limited knowledge of the language would not allow Brand to pick up her words. Whatever she was saying agitated Nante. The old man shook his head violently.

'I speak only American in the presence of my friend,' Nante said sternly. 'Do the same, Niana. While I still have life you will heed my words.'

The girl's shoulders stiffened, cheeks darkening with anger, yet she remained silent. Niana had spirit enough for two but she was a true Apache and did Nante's bidding.

'She does not believe you worthy,' Nante explained. 'Then she does not know you as I do.'

'She could be right, Nante. I'm no better than a hundred others. Even if I reach this secret place I might not pull it off. Maybe they won't listen to me.'

Nante reached out and clutched Brand's big fist, his own hand dwarfed by the American's.

'You have a way about you, Brand. You walk with violence. It is your life and it is the only thing Benito understands. It is the same with the white. Both are mad dogs who must be stopped. Is it not how it has always been, Brand? How we have lived our lives?'

Brand made no reply. There was no need. Nante understood him almost as well as McCord. They both were aware of his affinity to violence and his association with death. Even Brand had accepted that finality, though there were times when it repulsed him. He was a killer. His inborn skill, his one talent, was to destroy. Some epitaph.

He shook himself out of the somber mood as he realized Niana was watching him closely. It was as if she could read his thoughts. There was an odd expression in her eyes.

'Will you do this thing?' she asked.

'Yes.'

As Brand accepted the challenge he caught the ghost of a smile on Nante's withered face.

'I will get ready,' Niana said and left the hut.

26

'I have no need to thank you,' Nante said. 'Nor can I give you help. But take heed, Brand. Do not trust Benito. He is evil. He has used much *peyote*. It has poisoned his mind and many times a great madness comes over him. His rage is truly terrible. Never turn your back on him, Brand. Do what needs to be done and bring my people to San Carlos.'

'If it's possible I'll do that,' Brand promised.

Nante emptied his mug and held it out.

'Let us share one more drink, my friend.'

Brand took the mugs and crossed to the pot. He filled the mugs. As he replaced the pot he saw the fire had gone out. Crossing the hut he felt a chill touch his face and something made him kneel quickly beside Nante. The old Apache had sunk against the wall, eyes closed, and Brand knew the second mug of coffee would not be needed. Sadness gripped him for a moment. Nante had fulfilled his need to stay alive until Brand answered his summons. Now that had been done Nante, warrior of *The People*, had opened his arms to *Yussen* and had embarked on his final trek to the spirit world.

CHAPTER 3

Brand drifted across the dusty compound. Outside the administration building the US flag hung limply at the top of a white-painted pole. As he neared the low adobe building a laughing group of near-naked Apache children raced across his path. Their shrill cries barely penetrated Brand's deep thoughts. It was only as he reached the building that he became aware of the noise around him. He watched the playing children. Life for them was still a game, with little in the way of responsibilities.

Brand envied their innocence, though he knew it would soon be snatched away. As they played their childish games Niana wept over her dead grandfather. As one life ended others went on. It was the eternal way of things. Life and death, walking hand in hand under the sun. One day even his own life would end. Would anyone weep for him? The dark thought angered him. He snatched off his hat and scrubbed a big hand through his thick hair. He was getting morbid.

Sieber was seated behind his battered old desk,

drinking coffee. There was another man in the office, lounging in a cane-bottomed chair on the far side of the room. He was young, a tall, broad, good-looking man. The moment Brand met his gaze he felt himself go tense.

'Been a good long time, Jason.'

'Depends how you figure good,' Brand said.

Tom Horn grinned. There was little friendliness behind the smile. He and Brand had worked together before, but there had always been some wall of hostility between them. Brand could never explain the cause even when he tried to figure it out for himself. The plain truth of the matter was that he didn't like Tom Horn, despite the man's proven skill as a scout and Indian fighter. Horn was good at his job and had the requisite courage, but there was some hidden darkness in the man's make-up that got to Brand and made him see the other in a different light. Horn seemed to have a similar feeling towards Brand and whenever the two were together the atmosphere quickly became uncomfortable.

'Heard you lost that fancy marshal's badge,' Horn said casually as he stood up.

'Figured it was time I stood aside to let the others do something,' Brand replied. 'My problem is I don't know when to quit.'

'Weren't the way I heard . . .' Horn began.

'All right, you pair,' Sieber snapped. 'Last thing I need is you children playin' games. Tom, you got things to do. Get to it.' He turned to Brand. 'You sit. Cool off.'

Brand slumped in a chair and watched as Sieber

followed Horn to the door. When he returned he was scowling. He slammed the door, shaking his head as he stomped across the hard-packed floor.

'Like damn kids you are!' Sieber sank into his seat. 'Why bother! Should maybe let you fight it out. Feel better maybe if you blow holes in each other.'

Brand shrugged.

Sieber picked up his coffee mug. 'Want some?'

'No thanks, Al. I just had a cup with an old friend. Last one we'll share.'

Sieber caught the meaning behind the words.

'Nante? *Dead*?'

'Yeah.'

'By God, he meant it then. Said he'd stay alive long enough to talk with you. He do that?'

'Told me what he needed to.'

'You tell me?'

'Don't see why not. Nante wants his people to come to San Carlos and take the peace. He knew if they stay out they'll be hunted down. He wanted them safe. Trouble is one of his bucks has other ideas. Wants to keep the people on the trail. Seems this buck – Benito – is in with some white renegade who has a supply of guns and whiskey. All that won out over Nante's words.'

'So Nante wants you to go and bring his people in?'

'Something like that.' Brand grinned wryly. 'The old bastard was reminding him I owed him a favor.'

'And do you?'

Brand nodded.

'Time I went after a 'breed called Lobo I got into

31

a tight spot along the way. Nante turned up at the right time. Thinking on it I guess he saved my skin that day.'

Sieber grunted into his coffee.

'Nante tell you where his hideaway is?'

Brand shook his head.

'Niana knows. She's going to take me there.'

He stared out the window, across the compound. Heat waves shimmered in the still air.

'How long has she been here?'

'Six months or so. She just rode in one day and said Nante told her to come.'

Brand pushed to his feet and stood at the window. He was getting an uneasy feeling. He was committed now and his mind was starting to visualize the difficulties ahead. The trip into Sonora would be long and there was no way of knowing what he would find at the end of it. He was taking on unseen odds – not that it was a new situation for him. Any assignment he took on these days had unforeseen problems lurking in the shadows. If he was truthful he looked forward to the uncertainty. It made for an interesting life. Boredom was something he seldom experienced.

The door swung open wide and a dusty figure strode inside. Brand would have recognized the man anywhere. Dressed in a faded canvas jacket, with a shallow sun-helmet perched on his head, his forked beard streaked with dust he looked anything but what he actually was.

General George Crook, the man appointed to sort out the Apache problem in Arizona and New

Mexico, might not have looked the part but he was more than capable. His record in the field was excellent, and he had a grasp of the situation that was the envy of many lesser men. Crook was also a humanist. He saw the Apache as people, not as the animals some would have them judged. He took time to understand their problems and he was a willing listener. Crook preferred his Apaches alive and on the reservation, rather than dead. Not that he couldn't be a soldier when the need arose. When the time came he could hold his own against any odds. He had pursued raiding bands of Apaches into Mexico on more than one occasion and he was as expert in the field as he was at the conference table.

'Heard you were here,' Crook said. He crossed over to Brand and shook his hand. 'I knew Seiber would find you.' He slapped dust from his clothing as he crossed to a large clay *olla* and poured himself a cup of water. 'You look a little frayed around the edges, Brand, but apart from that no different from the last time I saw you.'

'Couple of years older, General.'

Crook smiled. He peered at Brand from beneath bushy brows.

'Did you get here in time?'

'Yes, sir.'

'Good man. Nante's a stubborn old devil. Wouldn't tell us a blamed thing. Even Sieber couldn't get a word out of him.'

Crook eased himself into a chair and looked at Brand with an expectant expression.

'Nante wanted me to go into Mexico and try to get

his people to quit fighting. It was why they'd kicked him out. Some young buck named Benito has taken charge. Seems he's backed by some white renegade. Nante was afraid his people would get themselves wiped out.'

'A fair appraisal of the situation, I'd say.' Crook pondered for a moment. 'Did he tell you how to find this stronghold of his in the Sierra Madre?'

'No, but he gave me a guide.'

'Who?'

'Niana.'

Crook glanced at Sieber.

'Nante's granddaughter. The girl who's been looking after him.'

Crook nodded. Turned back to Brand.

'Did you agree to go?'

'Crazy as it sounds I said yes.'

'Good man!' Crook sprang from his chair. 'I'm grateful, Brand. Time's critical. We're coming close to getting the top Apaches in for talks. There's a chance to make an agreement this time. As usual they're playing hard to get. Geronimo's got us running all over the blasted territory. He's testing me out. I think he'll come in but he wants to see how committed *I* am. I'll play his games if it'll get him round the table talking. One of the stumbling-blocks is Nante's old band. Small enough to make hit-and-run strikes. Well-armed and brutal in the extreme. They're causing trouble all down the line. My resources are already overstretched so I can't give you anything except all the supplies and equipment you need. And my profound thanks.'

'That'll do fine, General.'

'By the way, how is Nante? Any better?'

'He died a little while back, sir,' Sieber said. 'He stayed alive long enough to have his talk with Brand. Just like he said he would.'

Crook shook his head. 'I'm sorry about that. Nante was a real Apache. He should have had his time of peace.'

'I reckon he's got it, General,' Brand said. 'I figure Nante died at peace with himself and the world in general. He'd done his time and he was satisfied.'

'I hope so,' Crook said. 'He deserved it.'

They stood for a moment, silence filling the dusty room. From outside came the thud of hoofs, the jingle of harness, shouted commands. The moment was broken. Crook drained his cup of water and turned for the door, with Sieber close behind. Brand followed at a distance, preferring to be no more than an observer. He paused in the open doorway and watched the milling bunch of uniformed riders in the center of the compound. Part of Crook's command, they were a troop of blue-shirted soldiers who looked as if they had been in the saddle for the best part of a week – which they probably had. Men and horses alike were coated with sweat-soaked dust. Weariness showed in every move they made. Jason Brand wouldn't have traded places with them for $1,000 a month.

He felt the need for a drink that was a lot stronger than coffee. He made his way towards the cluster of buildings that stood apart from the main reservation. It was nothing more than a tiny village; a rundown *cantina*, a store and what passed for a livery stable. The majority of establishments were run by Mexicans. The *cantina* gave the impression it might fall down at any moment. It was empty save for the barkeep, a fat Mexican who was sweating just standing still. The man's eyes, small black marbles, were almost hidden by rolls of flabby skin.

'Whiskey?' the barkeep asked, making a weak attempt to swat a fly near his hand.

'You got *pulque?*'

Brand went and sat at one of the vacant tables, waiting to be served. He ran his gaze around the place. The grubby walls were streaked and peeling, the adobe turning soft and chalky. Even the air smelled moldy.

The Mexican waddled from behind the bar, bringing a squat clay bottle and a cloudy glass. He placed them both on the table. Brand had been staring out through the window beside his table. He could see the reservation. Even the hut where he'd spoken to Nante. He found himself thinking about the Apache girl, Niana, who would be performing the age-old burial ritual for the dead grandfather.

Brand picked up the bottle and poured himself some *pulque*. It was not as good as Sarita's brew. He pushed the thoughts from his mind, trying to clear his mind for what lay ahead. He concentrated on the bottle and what it contained and didn't break his concentration until he realized the bottle was empty. He ordered another.

The *cantina* had a few more customers now, a number of Mexicans.

And a pair of Americans. They caught Brand's attention. There was something about them that made him look closer. The first thing he noticed was the way they wore their guns. Not like working cowhands. More the way he carried his own weapon: like the tool of their trade. The Mexicans would have called them *pistoleros*. Men of the gun.

The pair were at the bar but facing his way, and Brand knew they were weighing him up.

But why?

Why should he be of any interest to them?

Draining his glass Brand shoved to his feet. He knew he'd had a little too much pulque on an empty stomach. He was feeling reckless. Belligerent. Knowing didn't stop him. He became aware of the two Americans' reaction as he closed in on them, and felt the old burn of excitement rising.

'You know me?' he asked brusquely.

His question took them off balance, and for a moment they were lost for words. One of them, tall and lean, with a honed edge to his brown face, recovered faster than his partner.

'Hell you talkin' about, mister?' He was attempting to cover up the fact that he'd been caught out. 'We just came in for a damn drink is all.'

'So you say. Only I get the feeling you've been paying more attention to me than to what you got in them glasses. Now why should I wonder about that?'

The second man found his voice.

'What's wrong with this *hombre*, Ed? He had too much to drink?' He was even less convincing than his partner.

Ed smiled without humor. He was like an actor who had suddenly forgotten his lines and had no one to prompt him. His gaze flickered towards the door, then back to Brand. He'd been working at a possible escape route and was fast realizing there wasn't one. The only way out was the hard one.

'*Damn you!*' he yelled, his frustration boiling over into unthinking action.

Brand saw the punch coming and easily side-stepped it. He felt the rush of air as Ed's fist slid by his cheek. Brand leaned forward and drove a hard fist deep into the man's flat belly. Ed grunted, falling forward against Brand, who shouldered him aside. As Ed stumbled Brand threw a hard backhand across the side of his face. The blow landed with a solid *whack* and Brand felt flesh tear. Blood spurted as Ed went down on his knees.

'*Hey!*'

The challenge came from Ed's partner. Brand turned to meet his attack and found he'd misjudged the man. Short, with broad shoulders, the man moved with surprising speed. His shoulder sledged into Brand's chest, sending him backpedalling across the floor. The edge of a table stopped him, turning him slightly, so that the heavy punch thrown at his face scraped across the line of his jaw. The impact was still solid enough to jar his senses. Brand shook his head, trying to clear the mist in his eyes, moving to distance himself from his opponent. He caught the flurry of movement and threw up his arm to block the fist sweeping in at him. At the same time he kicked out with his right foot, swinging a brutal kick that thudded against the other's side. Pain was expressed in a sharp yell as the impact of Brand's kick spun the man back against the bar. It rocked under his bulk. Recovered enough to gain control of his movements again Brand followed the man and slammed both hands against the back of his attacker's head. He put his full strength into slamming the stocky man face down on the bar top. A wet gurgle burst from his crushed mouth. Brand hauled him away from the bar and punched him hard. The man went down in a loose sprawl, bruised and bloody.

A rustle of sound made Brand turn. Ed was back on his feet. He had a knife in his hand.

'They never said you were that good.'

The words were more to himself, but they confirmed to Brand that his earlier suspicion had been correct. The pair had not been in the cantina by accident. He still couldn't figure out why – but he was starting to get the feeling it had something to do with his summons to San Carlos and Nante's request.

Ed made an ill-timed lunge, the knife curving in at Brand's stomach. He eased aside, the knife slipping by, and grabbed Ed's wrist before the man could recover. Pulling Ed in close Brand slid his other arm beneath Ed's, then levered up against the joint. Ed gasped. Despite the pain he had the presence of mind to make use of his free hand. Jamming the palm under Brand's jaw he shoved Brand's head back.

For a moment the pair swayed, each trying to gain the advantage. Brand felt himself being shoved against the edge of the bar, his spine crushed by Ed's weight. He hooked his left foot behind Ed's legs and put all he had into a forward thrust. Ed yelled out as he felt himself going back, losing his balance. The pair hit the floor hard, twisting and squirming. Somewhere in the struggle Ed lost his grip on the knife. Then he slammed a hard blow to Brand's cheek, spinning him across the floor.

As Brand scrambled to his feet, searching for Ed, he saw the man rushing forward. Ed had a heavy wooden stool in his hands and he was already half-way through a vicious swing. Brand tried to dodge out of the way but the edge of the stool caught him over the left eye. The blow drove Brand into the side of the bar. He bounced off and fell. He didn't remember hitting the floor.

CHAPTER 4

'*A reservation is there to promote peace and harmony,*' Al Sieber grumbled. He sat back, arms folded across his broad chest, watching Brand drain the mug of black coffee.

'Pity the pair I tangled with didn't have the same idea,' Brand said.

He raised his aching head and saw the room spin wildly. He wasn't feeling too steady. There was a darkening bruise over his left eye where the stool had hit him.

'Still don't know who they were?'

'No. But I'm damn sure they had something to do with Nante sending for me.'

Brand stood up and crossed to where the pot bubbled on the stove. He poured himself another mug, staring out the window, then turned to glare at Sieber.

'Let's face it, Al. If there are white renegades involved with Benito they won't want their game upsetting.'

'This deal get queerer by the minute,' Sieber

vowed. 'You goin' to have plenty trouble. Not even started yet an' already you got problems.'

'Anyone see that pair leave?'

'No. First we hear about is when you walk in dripping blood everywhere.'

'I'll be seeing them again, that's for damn sure. Al, I aim to head out at first light. Right now I could do with some sleep. You got somewhere I can bunk?'

Sieber nodded. 'Sure thing. There's room in back you can use. Don't worry about supplies. I arrange everything.'

'Thanks, Al. Tell Niana we leave in the morning.'

Sieber showed him to a small room which was furnished with a low cot and a chair. When he was alone Brand unbuckled his gun belt and laid it on the chair, the butt of the heavy Colt turned in towards the cot so he could get to it fast if the need arose.

The room had a square hole cut in the adobe that served as a window. Despite this the room was airless, the heat pressing in on him. Brand could feel his shirt sticking to his flesh so he peeled it off and lay down, closing his eyes. He tried to ignore the dull throb of pain inside his skull. He knew he'd been lucky. The blow from the stool could have resulted in something far more serious than a severe headache. *What the hell was he getting himself into?* No picnic, that was for sure. In the morning he was going to ride out for Mexico with an Apache girl, with little idea what he was going to find, or what he was going to do.

Maybe he was starting to go a little crazy. After all, only a short few days back he'd been safe and happy, lazing away his days with Sarita on her little farm. Now he had walked open-eyed back into the world of violence he'd been trying to distance himself from. He'd very nearly caught a knife in the ribs already, and when that didn't happen he'd taken a clout on the head with a damn bar stool. A man had to be half-way crazy to let himself in for that kind of treatment.

Then he thought back to Sieber's offer and the way *he* had fallen in with it right off. He had no one to blame except himself. He knew why. The smell of danger. The lure of excitement beckoning him had been too much to ignore. He'd known from the start that violent confrontation would be waiting somewhere along whatever trail he rode. And that was enough to reel him in. He just couldn't resist.

He rolled over on the cot, staring at the gun on the chair. And wasn't that part of it all? The gun. The tool of his trade. The cold steel that set him apart from other men. Brand reached out and touched the smooth butt of the weapon, and in the same instant he silently cursed the power it had over him. Would there ever be a time when he'd be able to exist without it? Deep inside he knew the answer was no – he was as dependent on his gun as any alcoholic on his bottle of whiskey. The frustration he felt came from this knowledge and his inability to break free.

He didn't even consider putting it to the test because he knew he would fail. It was his weakness and he would never conquer it. He despised his frailty; hated what it had done to him; the hurt it brought him and those who surrounded him. He damned the curse of the gun and what it had done to his life. Wishing he could be free was not going to change a damn thing. He was, and would remain, a *pistolero*. The shadow of his curse would follow him to the grave. No matter how far he ran, when he looked over his shoulder the shadow would always be there.

So why bother trying to fight it?

Sleep came slowly. Brand tossed and turned in the confines of that stuffy room. Even when he did fall into a restless slumber his mind was alive with disturbing images, shadowy and menacing, that beckoned to him, refusing him the peace he wanted more than anything.

He woke suddenly, aware that night had fallen, and he was filled with the knowledge that he was not alone.

Brand reached for the Colt on the chair. As he pulled it from the holster, snapping back the hammer, he sat upright. The muzzle of the Colt settled on the pair of dark figures standing against the far wall.

'You will not need the gun, Brand.'

It was Niana. She moved to the side of the cot and Brand made out the soft oval of her face as she broke through a shaft of pale moonlight.

'Will you promise not to give us away?' she asked.

Brand looked beyond her to the still silent figure by the wall. Darkness masked the features but Brand knew without doubt he was looking at an Apache.

'My word was always good enough for Nante.'

Niana spoke gently in her own tongue and the

waiting figure moved from the far side of the room as Brand stood to meet him. The Apache held himself erect, waiting. Brand studied the seamed, coppery face, the brittle eyes. There was something familiar about the man.

'Geronimo risks much to come and speak with you,' Niana said, her hand reaching out to grip Brand's arm. 'There is much danger here.'

'He'll be safe enough,' Brand promised. He eyed the stocky figure and the realization came to him that he was face to face with the most wanted Apache in the South-west.

Geronimo – the legendary leader of the Chiricahua Apaches. The man who had spread terror and destruction for years while the Army tried in vain to capture him. A brilliant tactician and a deadly fighter, Geronimo was both wise and wily. A man to be feared and respected. Jason Brand kept those thoughts in mind as he faced the Apache.

'Nante, my friend, is dead,' Geronimo said. 'My heart is heavy. Nante was a good Apache. We fought together many times. Now there is one less voice to speak for *The People*.'

'He was my friend too and I know he wanted peace for the Apache. Is this what Geronimo wants also?'

Geronimo's features hardened for a moment.

'It is hard to think of surrender. For many years we have fought and we have survived against the whites. Now the time is coming when the Apache must decide. Do we fight on and die. Or do we give ourselves over to the *Pinda Lickoyi* and hope he honors his promises. Many of our people want to keep fighting. But I have seen the women weep over their dead. And I have heard the children cry from hunger. Soon I will come and talk with Gray Fox.'

'Crook is an honest man,' Brand said. 'He will not deceive you. Talk with him, Geronimo. Make a peace for your people and hope for the future. It won't come easy. But it's better than being dead.'

'You were a good friend to Nante,' Geronimo said. 'When he asked you to come you came without question. Nante asked you to help his people. I ask this too. This crazy one – Benito – is making it hard for all Apaches who are thinking of surrender. As long as Benito kills and destroys it makes a lie of our words of peace. I know Benito. His hate is deep and the peyote has poisoned his mind to reason. He must be stopped, Brand, and also this white who gives him guns and whiskey. If you can do this then perhaps I will meet with Crook and we can talk peace.'

'I'll try. Can't say more.'

Geronimo stared at him for a long time, his eyes boring into Brand's. Then he nodded stiffly.

'The story is still told how you hunted down the one named Lobo and killed him. Any man who could do that is the equal of Benito. Word will reach me if you succeed or not. The right way will run its own course.'

Turning away Geronimo spoke a few words in Apache to Niana. Then he padded to the window, eased himself across the sill and vanished into the night.

Brand sat on the edge of the bed. He glanced at Niana, smiling.

'If that don't beat all,' he commented. He was thinking about Crook and Al Sieber, imagining their reaction if they knew Geronimo had been right in their midst. At the thought of seeing Sieber's face Brand couldn't help chuckling to himself.

'Why do you laugh, Brand?' Niana asked, her pretty face creased in a frown.

'You wouldn't understand,' Brand said. 'By the way, what did Geronimo say to you before he scooted out the window?'

Niana drew herself upright. Brand was sure he saw a flush on her cheeks.

'It was nothing,' she said softly.

'What was nothing?' Brand persisted.

'That I should see to your needs as any good Apache woman should for her man.'

Brand didn't press the point. He understood what Geronimo had meant. He watched Niana's face, still smiling slightly, and in the end the girl turned abruptly and left the room, closing the door with a solid bang.

Brand lay down, ready for sleep. All in all it had been one hell of a day. And there was still tomorrow to come.

CHAPTER 5

Ed Hamner watched the distant pair of riders through a shimmering heat haze. The only emotion he felt was one of relief. Hamner and his partner, Dan Yorrick, had been sitting on their pile of rocks since the previous night, waiting for the man called Brand to show. If Bigelow's information was right, and it usually was, Brand would be heading for the border and Sonora. His trail would bring him right by this place. Hamner didn't have the patience for such a long wait. He was no damned Apache, able to sit in one spot for days if necessary. Hamner needed action. Something to relieve the boredom.

He was too impulsive – he admitted to that – and it got him into trouble on a regular basis. Like the tangle with Brand back at San Carlos. He felt sweat break out at the memory. It had got close to the edge. Close enough to almost drag them all into a gunfight. Hamner didn't have any desire to face Brand's gun. He knew the man's reputation. Brand was one of those men who stayed calm during a face-off. He didn't lose control. Which was why he was able to walk away and leave his opponents on the ground.

Hamner glanced across at Yorrick. His partner looked as if he was asleep, his hat pulled down across his face to shield his bruises from the hot sun. Hamner didn't envy Yorrick's condition. His face was badly swollen. His nose was crushed almost flat and he'd lost a tooth. Both his lips were split and raw. The heat and dust were making life miserable for Yorrick. He was in a foul mood, so Hamner decided it was wiser to leave the man alone. Maybe Yorrick would cheer up once he knew the long wait was almost over.

Easing back from the rim of rock Hamner picked up his canteen and took a swallow. The water was brackish and warm, but it eased his parched throat a little. For a moment he wished the canteen was full of whiskey. He dismissed the thought. Out here in this damn country a man needed his wits about him. Especially if he was drifting towards a showdown.

Hamner picked up his rifle, glad now that he'd kept it under a shallow outcropping, away from the heat of the sun. He used his hand to brush away the fine layer of dust that had settled on the weapon. He'd had the Winchester for a long time, looking after it well, and he'd used it to kill a number of men. The rifle had never let him down yet. He cared for it as well as he did for the Colt on his hip. They were the tools of his trade and when the moment came he had to know the guns would respond instantly. His very existence depended on their performance. Whatever else he might be, Ed Hamner was no fool when it came to looking after his weapons.

Turning back to the rim he eased the Winchester to his shoulder and took a long sighting on the distant riders. He had no intention of doing any shooting at the moment. Brand and the Apache girl were still well out of range. Hamner was simply indulging himself. There was no hurry. San Carlos lay a long ways back. Yorrick and Hamner could take their time over this kill. Brand had a long ride ahead of him and his trail would take him across a wide territory of barren land. Bigelow didn't want Brand and the girl to reach their intended destination. It was what he was paying Hamner and Yorrick to prevent. He'd get his money's worth, but it would be done in Hamner's own time. When *he* was ready.

He tired of his game and turned to stare at Yorrick. On impulse he stretched out a leg and poked Yorrick in the side with the toe of his boot.

Yorrick jerked upright, his hand snatching for the gun on his hip. His slitted eyes touched on Hamner's grinning features and he slumped back with a low growl.

'What the hell you do that for? Times are you're a mean son of a bitch!'

'It's what makes me so likable,' Hamner said evenly. 'Just thought you might like to know who's passin' by.'

Yorrick scrambled up to the rim and stared out across the sun-blasted terrain. It was hard to see far through his watering, near-closed eyes, and the glare of the sun hurt them. Yorrick blinked furiously, frustration rising as he tried to focus on the distant riders. He was eventually able to make out Brand and

51

the Apache girl, Niana.

Anger rose, bile in his throat as Brand's image burned into his mind. It was going to give him a great deal of satisfaction to kill Brand. Pain flared in his battered face as a reminder of what Brand had done. Yorrick was not a man who forgave easily, and he had good reason to hate Jason Brand.

He grabbed up his rifle, cursing as the hot metal seared his fingers. Working the lever he jacked a shell into the breech and jammed the stock against his shoulder.

'Dan, put the damn gun down!' Hamner's voice reached him through a mist of rage that flooded his senses.

'*What?*' Yorrick glared at his partner. 'What you sayin'?'

'You ain't goin' to hit them from here. They's too far off. Hell, you might as well try to pee on 'em. Do as much damage and it'll save you a bullet.'

Yorrick continued to stare along the rifle's barrel. He muttered under his breath, angered because Hamner was right of course. Brand *was* way out of range. He spat in frustration and slid down below the rim, hugging the rifle to his body.

'*I want that son of a bitch!*' he said with feeling.

'Ease off,' Hamner told him. 'We'll get him. Ain't no need to rush. He's got a way to go. No people around. Just wide open spaces. All we got to do is bide our time and pick a spot.'

Yorrick grunted. He had to give it to Ed. He had the knack of looking ahead and spotting the snags before they got in the way. Hamner had patience. He could wait for as long as it took. Yorrick was the opposite. He wanted things to happen *now*. Waiting got to him. He admitted it was a bad fault because it got him into trouble more times than not. His gut feeling told him to get to Brand and kill him . . . and the girl. *What about the girl?* For an Apache she wasn't bad-looking. She'd have to die too . . . but maybe not right away. Yorrick felt a stirring in his groin. It would be a damn shame not to make the most of an opportunity. The thought gave him some comfort and he settled against the warm rock, content to wait it out, and conjured up a fantasy in his mind that had Niana as its focal point.

CHAPTER 6

Since leaving San Carlos, Brand and the Apache girl, Niana, had barely exchanged more than a half-dozen words. There seemed to be little between them. Brand had his own problems to mull over, while Niana appeared to be occupied with thoughts of her own. Brand was still coming to terms with the dramatic change in her appearance. The buckskin dress had gone, replaced by a faded multicolored blouse and tight buckskin pants. She also wore knee-length, traditional Apache moccasins: *n'deh b'keh*. She had cut away her long hair, leaving a ragged, shoulder-length cut with a red headband. Around her waist she wore a scarred, much-used gun rig, with short-barreled Colt .44-40 snug in the holster. Brand had seen belt and gun before. It had belonged to Nante. When Niana had first appeared in her new guise Brand hadn't recognized her. He thought she was an Apache boy – but he had quickly realized his mistake. No Apache buck had the kind of shape lurking beneath such manly clothing.

'I have ponies ready,' she had said. 'Where we go

a pony is better than a horse. Yours will be cared for until we return.' She allowed a wry smile to touch her lips. 'Will you be able to ride the Apache way?'

Brand had known what she meant. No saddle. Just a blanket and a single braided rope for a rein.

'I reckon I'll get by,' he had told her.

Outside she had everything ready. Ponies waiting. Each animal carried supplies and water skins. Niana had mounted up and sat waiting while Brand went for a final word with Sieber and General Crook.

'You all ready?' Sieber had asked. He peered at Brand across the rise of his saddle as he tightened slack cinch straps.

Brand nodded. He had caught sight of Sieber's young Apache scout watching him, and he had wondered what went on behind that expressionless face.

'You heading back to Fort Apache?'

Al Sieber grunted a curt response.

'Crook's got an itch in his ass telling him Geronimo's somewhere close by. Looks like we're going to spend the next few weeks chasin' shadows again.'

Brand had held back a grin. Crook didn't know just how right he was. He had to bite back the desire to tell Sieber about his nocturnal visitor.

The clatter of hoofs had drawn Brand's attention. He had turned as General Crook reined in close by.

'Brand. I wish you luck.'

'Thanks, General, I figure I'm going to need it.'

Crook had given one of his hearty laughs.

'You'll do it, Mr Brand. I have every confidence in you.' The General held back his impatient mount. 'Ready and waiting for you, Mr Sieber!' he boomed, reining about to join his waiting troop.

'Sometimes,' Al Sieber had said, 'just sometimes I wish he wouldn't be so damn cheerful about everything.'

'Take care, Al,' Brand had said, turning away.

Sieber's voice had reached him almost in a whisper.

'And you, boy. I want to see you again. Up and walking around.'

Brand had raised a hand in farewell. Despite the fact that Sieber's words had been well meant he had felt a momentary doubt cross his mind. He had pushed it aside. There had been little time to dwell on it as he approached the waiting ponies and the still figure of Niana. He suddenly spotted a tall figure standing in the shadowed doorway of the administration building.

Tom Horn.

'Got everything you need, Jason?' Horn's voice had held a faintly mocking tone.

Brand had felt the old hostility rise and he had glanced at Horn, not missing the challenge in the younger man's eyes.

'Least ways you won't get bored out there,' Horn had continued. 'Not with that little Apache ass to warm your blanket at night.'

Brand had turned. He had not made any abrupt movement and Horn had stepped aside as Brand walked by, into the building. The second he was inside Brand turned, so that as Horn strolled in, still with that arrogant smirk on his face, he was waiting. The moment Horn crossed the threshold Brand acted. He simply and solidly hit Horn, his big fist catching the unsuspecting man across the jaw. The force of the blow drove Horn to the floor, blood streaking his slack mouth.

'Stay out of my way, Tom,' Brand had said gently. 'Next time I might just have to kill you!'

And then he had walked back outside to where Niana waited. Without a backward glance he had mounted his pony and had led the way off the San Carlos reservation.

Looking at Niana now he wondered if she had heard what Horn had said. He didn't think it would have mattered much to her if she had. Niana had a strong spirit, something she must have inherited from Nante. It would take more than a sly remark to upset her.

'Did you know we are being watched?'

The sound of her voice cut through Brand's thoughts. He did not react, but simply asked:

'Where?'

'On the left,' she said. 'There are many rocks. I have seen two men waiting in them.'

'Apache?'

Niana gently shook her head.

'*Pinda Lickoyi*,' she told him.

Bran had seen the upthrust of rock rising from the baked earth like a massive rotted tooth. It lay well to their left, beyond rifle-range. He decided the best thing to do was keep riding. Whoever was in the rocks owned the only decent cover available. Brand scanned the way ahead, trying to locate some place that might offer similar protection for Niana and himself. There was nothing, the terrain in front of them lay flat and open. It was a case of acting as if they suspected nothing and kept on riding.

The next question was who?

Brand could only think of two likely candidates. The pair he had clashed with back at San Carlos. They had made it clear, though denying it, that they had more than a passing interest in him. It seemed likely that whatever their reason it would not have vanished. Someone, somewhere, wanted Brand watched – or something more drastic.

But why?

Had his summons to Nante's side caught the attention of unfriendly ears? It was possible. There were plenty of individuals around San Carlos – white and Indian, who might be easily persuaded to keep an ear to the ground. Someone was supplying Benito's Apaches with guns and whiskey. It was a profitable trade to be in, and whoever was behind the set-up did not need someone like Jason Brand poking his nose in. Brand didn't fool himself. He was known in this part of the country. So was his close friendship with Al Sieber and the late Nante.

Brand didn't let his speculation draw his attention from the matter at hand. He still favored finding a place where he and Niana might secure themselves some decent cover. He was beginning to feel overexposed out on this flatland. Off to their right, though a good distance away, the foothills of the Galiuro Mountains showed. Too far to be of any help.

'Start to ease west,' he said to Niana, and when the Apache girl looked at him he said: 'If I've got it right those two watching us are the same ones I fought with back at San Carlos. Doesn't take much figuring they haven't trailed us out here just to tell us funny stories.'

'They want to kill us?'

Brand nodded. 'I'm damn certain of it.'

'Then we should stand and fight!'

Her young face wore an expression that might have stopped a lesser man. Brand ignored it.

'Out here? Where they can keep us in their sights all the time? Look, I might be prone to picking up my gun somewhat on the quick side. Stupid I'm not. If there's a chance for us I want the odds in our favor as well. That means getting into those foothills. I'll feel a lot safer sitting behind a large rock. They stop bullets a sight better than a shirt front.'

He sensed Niana's stubborn nature forming more questions.

'Forget it, Niana. I don't have the time or the inclination to waste words over this. Just start moving west. Once they figure what we're up to they'll come running. When that happens and I yell, you hit that pony and just keep on riding. You hear?'

Niana, her back straight and stiff, stared at him for a while. Then her dark head acknowledged his words.

'I hear, Jason Brand.'

They rode on, gradually taking the ponies in a

gentle curve which set them on a course that would bring them to the foothills of the Galiuros. Brand kept the pace slow, though his mind was racing ahead, judging the distance they had to cover before they reached the safety of the rocky slopes. He tried to put himself in the place of the two men following them – *how soon would they figure out his move?* It depended on how fast their minds worked: whether they suspected he was deliberately making for the foothills. For all they knew this could actually be his line of travel. Even that wasn't going to hold them for long. Regardless of the reason he was heading for the foothills, it still boiled down to the fact that he would eventually reach cover. Once he did they would lose a good chance of taking him in comparative comfort out here on the flatland. A good man with a rifle could pick them off easily. And once they reached the rocky slopes the game would change pace. It could become a dragged-out seek-and-find conflict, with no clear cut conclusion.

The gap closed with agonizing slowness. By now their stalkers must have left the place where they had been waiting. Brand was starting to get an itchy spot right between his shoulders. He eased around, glancing over his shoulder, and his body stiffened.

He'd been right. They were coming and damned fast, too. A cloud of pale dust rose behind the hard-pushed horses. Brand lifted his rifle from where he had it across his thighs, working the lever. Niana's ears caught the sound and she looked across at him, then beyond. Her keen eyes spotted the riders.

'Go,' Brand snapped, making it clear there was no

time for questions or hesitation.

Niana responded to his command, drumming her heels into her pony's sides.

As her pony drew away from him Brand threw another quick glance over his shoulder. The pair were really pushing their animals, closing fast. He slammed in his heels and felt his sturdy pony respond. Niana was well in front, bending low across her pony's neck, urging it on to even greater speed.

The rising slopes seemed an eternity away. It was as if they were standing still, getting no closer. Brand expected the sound of a shot any second. He knew the pair behind would be within rifle-range soon.

He had only just registered the thought when the flat crack of a rifle shot sounded. He saw the bullet strike the hard earth off to his left, yards away. A second shot followed. This was even closer. Brand urged his pony on, lying forward across its neck, wishing he had the comfort of his saddle under him.

Out of the pall of dust left by Niana's pony he saw the shape of the rocks marking the slopes of the foothills. Brand swung his pony into the maze of dun-colored rocks. He heard the whipcrack of another rifle shot. The bullet whined off a nearby boulder, peppering his face with needles of stone. Brand kept on riding, pushing deeper into the rocks. Ahead of him he could see Niana weaving in and out of the rocks. Shots were following with regularity. Sooner or later one of those bullets was going to find a target.

Brand yanked his pony to a halt, pulling it behind a large boulder. He slid off its back, using precious seconds to familiarize himself with his surroundings. To his right lay a steep shale slope. He ran towards it, digging in his heels as he started up the loose side. Reaching the top he dropped flat, eyes scanning the area below him.

He saw movement at the edge of a high boulder. He waited until the movement resolved itself into the shape of a man on foot. *A man with a rifle.* Brand already had his own weapon to his shoulder. He picked his target, held, then fired twice. His first shot missed by a fraction. The second caught the man in the right shoulder, knocking him back a few steps. The hit man dropped his rifle, cursing loudly at the pain in his shoulder, then lost his footing and fell. He hit the ground hard, twisting over on to his stomach as he struggled to climb to his feet. His right arm hung loosely at his side, blood spreading across his shirt. The exit wound was large and ragged, bloody strips of flesh and splintered bone showing. As he tried to get up the man was reaching for his holstered gun. He found it and began to pull it from the holster, but Brand's third shot crashed out and hit him in the lower back. The man skidded forward on his knees, then flopped face down on the ground.

Brand pushed to his feet and ran along the rim of the shale slope, seeking a fresh position. The downed man's partner would be around somewhere, and unless he was deaf, dumb and blind, he would have Brand's former position marked now.

And he had. A rifle blasted from below. The bullet sliced across Brand's left side. He felt the red-hot burn of the wound and the sudden spurt of blood.

He dropped to the ground, keeping below the rim of the slope, touching a hand to the place where the bullet had nicked him. As with most superficial wounds it was bleeding heavily. His hand came away wet and red and he wiped it against the leg of his pants.

It had fallen quiet. Brand lay still, listening. The sun burned the back of his neck. His mouth was dry and a chunk of rock was digging into his hip. He eased the offending stone from beneath his body and tossed it aside. He was starting to sweat, his shirt sticking to his back. He didn't relish the idea of remaining where he was for too long. Once his body had given up its natural moisture he was going to feel it. Dehydration was not a pleasant thing. His only consolation was that his adversary would be in the same position.

He heard the sound then. Very faint. He might have missed it if his ears hadn't been tuned for such a happening. Someone was on the move. It showed that his opponent didn't have a great deal of patience. The sound repeated itself a few seconds later, the dry, whispered sound of boot leather scraping lightly over rough stone.

Brand didn't move. He waited and listened and watched. He wanted his man in the right place before he made *his* move. This was the part of the game where there was only one chance. Waste it and you did not get another.

Four – maybe five – minutes dragged by. Brand's rifle grew hot in his hands. Even though he wasn't moving sweat was trickling down his face and he had to keep brushing it from his eyes.

Somewhere to his left a clumsy foot dislodged a stone. It rattled against other stones and started a minor and very brief slide of loose material. A thin smile touched Brand's lips. He remained still, letting the other man come to him. All he had to do was move the muzzle of his rifle round to where his stalker would show. He figured another minute should do it. He was only seconds out. First came the tip of a hat, followed by a hand reaching to gain a final grip. Then a man's head appeared. He wasn't even looking in Brand's direction. There was enough for Brand to recognize the man. It was one of the pair he had tangled with back at the reservation.

The one named Ed.

Unaware of Brand's close presence Ed Hamner dragged himself to the rim of the slope. Once he was over the top he would have a better view. The man named Brand had to be close by. Hamner was positive he had hit Brand with his last shot. He didn't think he had killed the man but he was certain he had wounded him. Something made him look back over his shoulder to where his partner lay. Hamner didn't feel much in the way of pity for Yorrick. The man had always been the same. Always bulling in before he had weighed the odds. Hamner had always been telling him that one day his lack of caution would get him killed. Yorrick never got the message – until today, and now it was too late. Hamner shook his head. Yorrick wouldn't make that mistake again.

Brand was thinking about mistakes at that very moment. He was thinking about the one Ed Hamner was making. The man had made his way up the slope carefully enough, but that one dislodged stone had been his undoing, and Brand would use that against him.

'Hey, Ed,' Brand said softly. He didn't need to raise his voice because Ed was that close.

A cold chill rose in Hamner's stomach. His muscles tensed as if a giant, icy hand had gripped him. He felt a cold, clammy sweat break out over his body. He knew without looking that he had been caught out. His assumption that Brand had been wounded and weakened had been a mistake, and he cursed himself for doing more or less what his partner had been guilty of. As he had climbed the slope he had congratulated himself on his smart move. He was going to sneak up and surprise Brand, finishing the man before he had a chance to retaliate. If it hadn't been so serious Hamner might have seen the funny side. In his present situation humor was the last thing on his mind. He was thinking that he had been stupid to think he could outwit Brand. The man's reputation was well known. He was a hard man, with a deadly skill, and he took no prisoners. Brand played for keeps, allowing nothing to stand in his way.

Knowing this Ed Hamner figured that if he was going to die, then at least he would go down trying.

He made his play, snatching his rifle round on Brand, and saw that the other had his own rifle already targeting him. Hamner let out a wild, despairing yell, still trying to bring his rifle on line.

Brand touched his trigger. His rifle kicked back as

it slammed out its shot. The bullet hit Hamner full in the face, to punch through his skull and out the back. There was a burst of bloody bone and flesh. Hamner was pushed back by the force of the bullet. He arched over, falling back down the slope in a cloud of dust that trailed after him. He rolled to the bottom and lay still, dead before the last of the stones had rattled around his body.

Brand stood up. His side hurt wickedly. It was still bleeding, though not as much. He made his way back to where he had left his pony and unhooked his water skin. He took a drink, swilling his face with a little of the tepid water.

'Niana, you can come out now,' he said. 'It's all over.'

The Apache girl appeared instantly. She had her revolver in her hand and Brand was sure she had been ready to use it. There was an angry scowl on her face.

'I have not been hiding,' she snapped at him, eyes blazing. 'I am Apache, granddaughter of Nante. Not a coward.'

Brand had to grin at her. It only made her more angry.

'Let's go look at our friends,' he said. 'See if we can learn anything from them.'

CHAPTER 7

Hamner was dead, but the other man was still alive. He was losing a lot of blood very quickly, and Brand knew he would be dead in a few minutes.

'Jesus Christ, it hurts,' Yorrick moaned through bloody lips. His face twisted in agony as Brand turned him over. He stared up at Brand, eyes filled with the pain of his wounds. 'You son of a bitch. I should have killed you back at San Carlos when Ed laid you out with that stool.'

'First lesson,' Brand said. 'Don't waste your chances. You learned it too late, and it's about to bury you.'

Yorrick cursed wildly. 'Sonofabitch. Don't figure on it being finished. Bigelow won't let go now he has his teeth in you.'

Brand glanced at Niana.

'Mean anything?'

'I heard Nante speak of a man named Bigelow. A *Pinda Lickoyi* who sells guns to the Apache. A man who will do anything for money.'

Yorrick clutched Brand's sleeve.

'You might have a name, friend, but you ain't got the man. Bigelow is smart. Damn smart.'

Brand knocked the hand aside.

'He can't be that smart. Not if he hired you and your partner. He should have gone for professionals.'

'*The hell with you...*' Yorrick stopped in mid-sentence, his eyes clouding over. A soft, rattling breath escaped his lips. Brand felt him go slack.

Brand pushed to his feet and crossed to his pony. He glanced at Niana.

'You any idea where this Bigelow hangs out?'

'A small town on the border. We can reach it in two days. Do you wish me to take you there?'

Brand picked up his pony's trailing rein.

'Yeah. I want to meet Mister Bigelow. I've got a feeling he's likely to be out of business very soon.'

Niana was not quite sure what he meant, but she was sure it meant trouble for someone. As she mounted her pony and fell in behind Brand she thought of the dead men they were leaving behind, and she realized now why Nante had chosen this man. If anyone could stop Benito and the *Pinda Lickoyi* who were helping him, it was surely this tall, dark-haired man who said little but killed like an Apache. She was sure that this Jason Brand was one who knew Death as closely as any man knew himself. He was of that breed who walked a lonely trail through life. He had known much bitterness and suffering. It showed in his eyes. Yet she knew that beneath the flesh lay the real spirit of this man. He appeared cold and unfeeling but there was more to him than that.

They stayed with the foothills until dark. Niana knew her way around this part of the country, and as the sun slid below the horizon she brought them to a secluded place among the high rocks where an underground spring fed a wide rock-pool with fresh, cool water. There was even a little grass sprouting from the crevices between the bleached stones around the pool. Brand decided he was going to have to rethink his way around the territory. This was one water-source he had never seen before. He didn't doubt that Niana probably knew of a fair number of these hidden places. Secret springs and pools known only to the Apache.

He picketed the ponies, then took his rifle and walked to a section of high ground. The land spread before him, a mottled green-and-brown blanket, now pooled with the deepening shadows of evening. He wondered if there was anyone else out there? Most likely Apaches, if anyone. Geronimo maybe? With Crook and Sieber on his trail? Sitting there, staring into the coming darkness, the thought came to him that it was all a crazy game. Life was slipping by for so many people and all they did was run around chasing each other from one end of the territory to the other.

And for what?

Was anything ever fully resolved by it all? The so-called victories by the whites over the Indians were all hollow. The Indians would be moved far from their natural surroundings to satisfy the whites and placed on some mangy, godforsaken piece of land not worth a cent, and there they were expected to live in peaceful contentment. The expectation was that they should be satisfied with their lot and grateful to the generosity of the white man. Brand had no illusions about his fellow man. A great many of them were grasping and greedy, interested in lining their own pockets and to hell with anyone else. Once they got their hands on Indian lands they fell to arguing among themselves over what should be done with it. In the end it all came down to those who had nothing trying to take it from those who had.

Brand pushed to his feet, easing the stiffness from his body. Damned if he wasn't doing too much thinking. He turned back down the slope and saw the soft glow coming from a small fire Niana had lit. A gentle night breeze carried the smell of coffee and something that smelled pleasantly like bacon. Niana glanced up as he reached the fire. She did not speak. Brand hunkered down across the fire from her and watched as she filled a tin plate with thick slices of bacon and spiced beans. She passed it to him. As he began to eat she filled a mug with coffee and placed it at his side. Then she took her own food, standing up to move away.

'You going somewhere?' he asked.

'It is not for the woman to eat with the warrior,' she told him.

'Is it done for her to obey his words?'

'Yes.'

'Then get yourself back here and don't let me hear any more talk like that.'

Niana returned and sat cross-legged, regarding him with curious eyes. He stared back at her. In the wavering glow of the fire her features took on a coppery tone. Her hair showed blacker than before, framing her face and lending it a startling beauty that surprised and pleased him.

'You are a strange one,' she said suddenly. 'I do not understand you.'

'What's there to understand. I'm a man doing his job. Nothing fancy about that, no different from a hundred others.'

Niana placed her plate on the ground. She shook her head.

'With you it is different, Jason Brand. You cannot live any other way. For you there is nothing else. You could not become a farmer who lives off the land. Or a man who works in a store.' She shook her dark head. 'I know you could not do these things, Brand. They would kill you faster than any bullet.'

Brand drained his coffee and reached for the pot, burning his fingers on the hot metal.

Damn these women, he thought. *Give one five minutes and she would take a man apart to see what made him tick. Even this Apache was the same.* He filled his mug and slammed the pot back on the fire. He could feel Niana's eyes on him and sensed the faint glow of amusement that sparkled in those dark pupils. The annoying thing was that she had been right on target.

'Tell me about Benito and *peyote.*'

His question was a way of changing the subject as well as a chance to ask about something that had been chafing away at the back of his mind. 'First I ever heard of peyote doing permanent harm.'

'*Peyote* has been used for many years,' Niana said.

'It brings visions to those who use it. It makes them happy. They dream of good things and when the peyote wears off there is no harm. But it is different with Benito. My grandfather told me of the time Benito drank much bad whiskey. It made him very sick and he almost died. The whiskey did something to him here,' she touched the side of her head. 'When he took *peyote* after this it made him crazy. He would remain so for many days after. It was as if the Evil Spirits were inside his head making him do wild things. Now he takes *peyote* all the time and *The People* are afraid of him. They fear him but they also believe he is possessed and they dare not touch him.'

'Well, the only spirit that ever got hold of me came out of a bottle,' Brand said. 'Seems to me it's time we put the cork back on Benito's magic potion.'

Niana frowned. 'Sometimes you speak in a strange tongue, Jason Brand, and then I do not understand you.'

Brand took off his gun belt. He unrolled his blankets and laid them on the still-warm ground. His handgun and rifle were placed close by.

'Niana, let's sleep on it,' he said.

He lay down and pulled his blanket over him. He watched as the stars began to show. Close by he could hear the sounds Niana made as she took the plates and utensils down to the pool to wash them. Soon even those sounds ceased and it became very quiet. Brand was starting to drift off into sleep when a gentle hand touched his shoulder. He opened his eyes and in the faint glow from the fire he recognized Niana's face.

'The water is cold,' she said softly. 'And the fire is very small.'

Brand eased up on one elbow. He saw that Niana was naked. He reached out to touch her smooth shoulder. The brown flesh was cool and damp. His gaze dropped to the taut shape of her young breasts. The dark nipples were stiff from the cold water. Soft fingers of firelight played across the muscled smoothness of her torso and flat belly. At the junction of her strong thighs a dark triangle of hair showed, shadowed and mysterious.

Brand raised his blanket and Niana slid in beside him, pushing her firm body against his. He drew the blanket around them both, pulling her close. He felt the warm press of her thighs against his groin, became aware of his own swift response. He drew a firm hand across her shoulder and down to the swollen tip of one hard, warm breast. Her nipple was full and hard, and a soft sound bubbled from her throat as he caressed her. Nimble fingers loosened his shirt and eased it from his shoulders. Her tender touch explored his scarred, muscled body, touching the place where Hamner's bullet had gouged his flesh, and she felt his involuntary shudder.

'Why did you not tell me it pained you?' she asked.

He kissed her cheek.

'Tell you what,' he said. 'Damned if I can feel anything paining me at all.'

He searched for her mouth and felt her draw back. A wry smile curved his lips. Kissing would be something new to her. It was not really part of the Apache way.

'Is this how the *Pinda Lickoyi* love?' she asked.

'We show affection by it.'

She pushed closer, her naked flesh warm and inviting.

'Show me your way, Brand.'

Her initial hesitation quickly turned to eager exploration. Niana found growing pleasure in these new sensations. She was a willing pupil. One who adapted to the situation with increasing passion.

'This is a good way,' she announced some time later.

Brand didn't speak. His lips were becoming decidedly numb. It was almost a relief when he felt Niana's nimble fingers tugging at his belt buckle so she could loosen his pants, so she could reach his aching manhood. She held him firmly, the caressing proving she was not a beginner in this area. Her twisting and turning brought her beneath him and her spreading thighs told him better than words what she wanted. He entered her easily, his first thrust taking him deep inside her soft, moist flesh. Niana closed her taut thighs around him, gasping at the depth of his penetration. He felt her youthful body arching up off the ground, responding to the stimulation. He drew himself close, pushing hard. Almost too soon he felt her trembling in the throes of her release. His own came quickly and he clung to her, shuddering in the aftermath. As they sank into the closeness of their passion, feeling the strength draining from them, Brand hoped they might have another opportunity to experience what had just happened.

Niana turned her face to his, touching his cheek,

her soft mouth searching for his.

'Again, Brand,' she said. 'Again.'

Her mouth bent against his, hungry and demanding, and he wondered which would wear out first – her desire for this new experience, or *his* lips.

CHAPTER 8

Brand took his time studying the tiny spread of buildings which comprised the nameless settlement where, according to Niana, the man named Rafe Bigelow ran things *his* way. It seemed, Brand decided, that Bigelow was the way and the light. Niana's telling had the man down as a real hell-raiser. Brand figured he would decide for himself. He didn't really give a damn who Bigelow thought he was.

In the time it had taken them to reach the place, with the border only a couple of miles away, he and Niana had ridden in a wide loop that took them east and then in a long curve that brought them in from the west. Brand didn't want it to look as if they had ridden in from San Carlos, or had any connection with Hamner and Yorrick. He was well aware that his deception might not work and Bigelow would know who they were, but it was a chance he was going to have to take. Now he was here he wanted time to look it over; not that there was a great deal to see.

From their position on the low ridge Niana

pointed out the various buildings. Brand's main interest centred on the low, wood-and-adobe structure that made up Bigelow's headquarters. It fronted as a store-cum-trading-post, the kind of enterprise that proliferated in the frontier country. In the sparsely populated territories, where a man might have to ride for days before he saw anything remotely resembling civilization, outfits like Bigelow's could often be life-savers. Apart from the chance to talk to other human beings there would be the chance to stock up on food and other essentials.

According to the stories, Bigelow offered just that and more. If that was true Brand needed to locate the illegal goods. After he had, what then? Brand decided he would find a way around that problem when it showed.

He stood up, moved away from the ridge and returned to where the ponies waited. Niana followed him and hunkered down on her heels in the dust, her dark eyes studying him intently as Brand checked his weapons.

'Wait here,' he told her. 'If things get rough I don't want to be worrying about you all the time.'

Niana didn't reply. From the back of his pony Brand glanced down at her. Her head was down and she appeared to be studying the dirt between her feet.

'Could be someone down there who might recognize you. I need to get my foot in the door before some nervous type starts shooting. You understand?'

Her only response was a slight shrug. Brand grinned. He turned the pony about, pushing it up the slope and over the ridge. Silence closed around him as he rode down the far side. Dust feathered the air in his wake. In the heat haze Bigelow's headquarters might have seemed to be deserted but Brand guessed he had been spotted once his pony reached the flats that took him in towards the place. In Bigelow's line of work it didn't pay to run a loose ship.

As he got closer he began to make out details. A weathered sign over the door read: TRADING POST. SUPPLIES. LIQUOR. At the side of the building he saw a smaller hut and a split-pole corral holding a bunch of dusty, listless horses. Barrels and packing-cases littered the rear of the building. When he looked beyond Bigelow's building the rest of the settlement presented a similar picture; seedy and run-down; almost careless of its own existence.

Brand brought his pony to a halt at the hitching rail. As he slid off its back he spotted a lean figure lounging on a wooden bench close to the open door. Brand noticed the holstered gun the man carried. It was worn on his left hip, butt forward and it wasn't there for show. It wasn't a surprise. Bigelow would need insurance. As he moved in towards the door Brand saw that the lean man no longer lounged. He was on his feet, full attention on the new arrival.

Brand tied his pony and made for the open door. His rifle was in his left hand, leaving his other free if he needed the heavy Colt.

The lean man eased forward.

'You got business here?'

'You Bigelow?'

81

The man shook his head. Brand stepped around him.

'Then we ain't got business.'

'I'll decide that.'

Brand faced him, his stance relaxed.

'I came to see Bigelow. Hired hands don't interest me.'

A muscle twitched in the lean man's jaw. Breath hissed through tight-clenched teeth. His right hand eased towards the smooth worn butt of the holstered revolver he carried.

Brand stepped in close, swinging the rifle he was holding. The hard stock cracked against the lean man's jaw, splitting the flesh and spinning the man round. He was still moving when Brand struck again. This time he laid the stock hard behind the man's ear. The gunman grunted, stunned by the blow. He fell to his knees, then sagged forward, trying to catch himself by throwing out his hands. His strength had drained away, he fell face down in the dust and lay still. Brand bent over the prone figure, took the man's gun and tossed it towards the corral.

He turned then to carry on towards the door again.

And found it was completely blocked by a massive figure. The man was as tall as Brand but twice as wide. None of his bulk was made up of fat. It was all solid muscle.

'Bigelow?' Brand asked.

The large head nodded. 'You want to see me?'

'That's right. I figure maybe we can do some business.'

Mentally Brand was warning himself to step carefully with Bigelow. The man looked as if he could handle himself.

'That's what I'm here for,' Bigelow said, studying Brand as he spoke. 'What kind of business?'

'I'm selling,' Brand said.

He saw the hard gleam in Bigelow's cold eyes. Caution must have been the man's middle name. Thinking about it Brand decided he would have been the same given Bigelow's line of business.

'What you peddling, mister?'

Brand held up his rifle.

'These.'

'Talk like that could get you a bullet in the back of the head, friend. Don't you know the army ain't partial to folk who deal in guns?'

Brand smiled. 'I hear tell it doesn't worry you much.'

'Man shouldn't believe everything he hears.'

'I make up my own mind.'

Rafe Bigelow stepped back inside his store.

'Let's talk. Make sure we both know what we're into.'

Brand followed him inside. The interior was dim after the sun-bright day, but not so dim that Brand could not see the two figures standing in the shadows to one side of the door. Bigelow nodded to them.

'Go pick Delta up. Toss him in the trough. I pay him to do a job. Streak of piss couldn't keep an old lady out.'

Brand trailed after Bigelow through the cluttered store. The store was crammed with pretty well everything anyone could ever need out here. There was even a crude bar set up against one wall, with shelves holding bottles, and a large oval mirror with a crack in it. Bigelow booted open a door and lumbered into a room that served as his office. He thrust his huge bulk into a large leather chair behind a scarred wooden desk and waved Brand into another seat.

'Talk, friend, and make it good.'

Brand laid the rifle on the desk.

'I been trading with the Apache on and off. Done a few deals with old Geronimo hisself. Trouble is business ain't so good any more. Most of the tribes are for quittin'. Geronimo has it on his mind too. Told me a few days back when I showed him what I had. He's been talking with Sieber and it looks like Geronimo has more or less made up his mind. Word is you got the market pretty well to yourself these days.'

'What do they call you, friend?'

'Jack Taylor,' Brand said.

'Well, Taylor, what you say might be true enough. Then again you might be feeding me a crock of shit. And I wouldn't take kindly to that.'

Brand cuffed his hat back.

'Bigelow, I don't have all day to sit here playing guessing games. Let's quit foolin' around. We both know you trade whiskey and guns to the Apache. I got two cases of brand new Winchesters that got diverted from the warehouse they were heading for. There are four boxes of ammunition as well. If you want to deal let's get on with it. If you don't I'll trail on over the border and find me some Mexicans.

They'll buy without all the questions.'

Rafe Bigelow placed his large hands on the desk top and leaned forward. His lips drew back to reveal a yellow-toothed smile.

'I ain't heard such a mouthful in a long time, Taylor. Talk like that must leave a powerful thirst. You want a drink?'

'Yeah.'

Bigelow stood up and left the office. When he returned he carried a couple of clay jars.

'You like *pulque*?'

'About as much as I like Mexican ladies,' Brand told him.

He took the jar Bigelow offered and tried the drink. It was a fair brew but not as smooth as the pulque Sarita had provided.

'You got your merchandise handy?' Bigelow asked, sleeving away the *pulque* that ran down his massive chin.

Brand grinned. 'Do I look that simple? I got those rifles where I can get to 'em fast. But not until I got me a square deal.'

Bigelow laughed out loud. 'Damned if we should-n't get on, Taylor. Ain't neither one trusts the other. It's the only way to do business.'

They finished the jars of *pulque*. Bigelow brought two more. While the big man drank greedily Brand took his time. He had no intention of getting drunk. He didn't give a damn if Bigelow drank too much. The *pulque* was starting to loosen his tongue. When Bigelow saw that Brand was still on his first he grabbed the second jar he had brought for his guest and started on that one. They indulged in a round of small talk, then Brand slowly brought the conversation round to Bigelow's cache of weapons.

'Must be a hell of a job keepin' 'em hidden from the army.'

Bigelow was half-slumped across the desk, grinning from ear to ear. He waved a loose hand in dismissal.

'Those bastards in blue are so damn stupid they ain't got an idea.' He gave a snorting laugh. 'Listen, Taylor, I've had me army boys right where you're sitting and they didn't realize they were on top of enough powder and shot to blow their asses clear to Sonora.'

Under the floor. A damned cellar. Brand kept his face impassive as he digested Bigelow's words. He toyed with his jar of *pulque*, suddenly aware that Bigelow was staring at him hard. It was as if the man had realized what he had said and it had sobered him instantly. The big man cleared his throat and sat upright.

'Maybe I'd better get one of the boys to ride out with you, Taylor. Take a look at those guns. I need to know I ain't being sold a pile of junk. You figure I'm bein' fair?'

'I guess so.'

Brand stood up, watching Bigelow closely. The man didn't wear a gun but that didn't mean he was harmless. Brand only had to take a look at the massive arms bulging with hard muscle, straining against the sleeves of his shirt, to remind him of Bigelow's powerful physique.

'Let's go,' Bigelow said, leading the way back to the main store.

Brand followed, playing along for the moment. He needed to know the odds against him. He had no way of knowing just how many men Bigelow had around the place apart from the three he had already seen.

Outside the store Brand saw Delta slumped on his bench. He was holding a bloody cloth against the side of his head. When he saw Brand he made an attempt to push to his feet, scowling with anger. Bigelow reached out and pushed him back down again.

'Leave it, Delta. This ain't the time.'

Delta sat down again, still scowling, his eyes fixed on Brand.

Bigelow called one of his men from inside the store.

'Vern, you take a ride with Taylor. He's got some rifles for you to look at. I like to know what kind of deal I'm buying into. Right, Taylor?'

Brand nodded to the man named Vern as he stepped outside. Behind him was the second man Brand had noticed inside the store. He caught Brand's stare, returning it with a hard look.

Bigelow turned his attention to this man.

'Ryker, you stay here with Delta and me.'

Brand crossed to where his pony stood and Vern headed for the corral to pick up his own horse.

The man called Ryker muttered: 'When the hell are Hamner and Yorrick gettin' back? Leaves just the four of us.'

Brand heard his words and silently thanked Ryker.

Just the four of them. Bigelow, Ryker, Vern and Delta. What Ryker didn't know was that Hamner and Yorrick were not coming back.

Reaching his pony Brand started to pick up the reins. His move was stopped when he heard Ryker suddenly yell.

'*Goddam it*! I knew I'd seen that face before. Just come to me. Bigelow, he ain't anyone called Taylor. It's the sonofabitch Hamner and Yorrick went after. Brand! Saw him once when he was a US marshal!'

In that split second Brand ducked under his pony's neck, yanking his Colt free and dogging back the hammer. He dropped down on one knee, aiming beneath the pony's stomach. He saw Bigelow's huge form vanish back inside the store. Vern had already turned away from the corral, reaching for his holstered Colt. The one called Ryker had his gun in his hand, and Delta was pushing up off his bench like a striking rattler.

Brand's first shot took Ryker, blasting a bloody hole in his chest. The force of the .45 caliber bullet spun Ryker round. He slammed into the adobe wall of the store, blood spraying in a wide arc from the ragged wound in his back where the bullet had emerged. As he started to go down he fell in front of Delta, causing the gunman to step back, giving Brand the moment of time he needed to shift his aim. Before he could fire Brand's pony reared away from the hitch rail, slamming into Brand and knocking him to the ground. The incident saved Brand's life. The fall took him away from Delta's first shot. Spitting dust from his mouth Brand pushed his right arm forward, raised the barrel of his Colt and triggered two quick shots through Delta's lean body. Delta fell back as if he had been kicked by a mule, arms waving helplessly, a look of surprise on his face. His legs went from under him and he crashed to the ground. He made soft grunting sounds as blood bubbled from his open mouth. He pawed at his torn chest, fingers trying to stem the spurts of blood erupting from the bullet wounds.

The moment he had fired at Delta, seeing his shots find their target, Brand moved, rolling to a fresh position. As he came to rest he heard a shot and felt a bullet burn his left shoulder. Pushing to his feet Brand turned to face Vern, his already cocked gun levelling. He felt the familiar kick-back of the butt in his hand. Saw the bullet hit Vern low on the right side. Dust blossomed from Vern's shirt, followed by a spread of blood. Vern kept on coming and Brand had to put two more bullets into him before he went down for good. Vern's final shot had scored across the back of Brand's left hand and he dropped his rifle.

Brand wiped away the blood on the back of his hand and picked up his rifle. He levered a round into the chamber as he made for the door of the store. Delta was struggling to push up off the ground, coughing blood as he fought to control his gunhand. He looked up at Brand, spitting blood.

'Sonofabitch,' he said.

'Got that right,' Brand said and shot him through the head.

Brand took the time to reload his Colt, standing

with his back to the adobe wall close by the open
door. He preferred the Colt for close work. Brand
didn't relish going inside the store after Bigelow but
it needed to be done now. Bigelow was under threat.
His life and his business were at risk and Brand
didn't see the man as one who would quit easy.

He waited, minutes slipping by. It was too quiet,
Brand decided. What the hell was Bigelow up to?
Impatience began to insist Brand did something.
The bullet-grazes across his shoulder and hand were
making their presence felt.

Brand made his decision.

If you ain't coming out, Bigelow, I'll have to come in.

He moved away from the wall, his attention
focused on the open door. Then he registered the
rippling hiss of sound behind him. He started to
turn. He wasn't fast enough. There was a sharp crack.
Almost like a pistol shot. Pain engulfed his right
hand. The pain was intense. Brand felt flesh tear,
blood coursing through his fingers. He lost his grip
on the Colt and it fell to the ground.

Brand turned about completely, coming face to
face with Rafe Bigelow.

He saw too the eight-foot black bullwhip coiled in
the dust at Bigelow's feet. The sight of the long coil
of the whip sent a cold shudder along Brand's spine.

Bigelow's arm jerked back and the long, oiled
length of the whip curved behind him. Knowing he
only had seconds left to him Brand turned, his eyes
searching frantically for the Colt he had dropped. It
lay no more than a couple of feet from him and he
bent forward, reaching for the weapon, blood drip-

ping from his hand. He had barely stroked the curve of the butt when he heard that sinister hissing sound again. The lash of the whip coiled around his right arm, drawing more burning pain as it sliced through his shirt and scored his flesh. Blood flowed and a groan slipped from Brand's lips. He felt the sudden pull of the whip, snagged tight around his arm and he was twisted around to face Bigelow. The big man made a sharp movement and the whip uncoiled itself. Bigelow swept it back, then lashed out again. The black, splayed tip of the whip stung Brand's cheek, opening a gash that streamed warm blood. Sharp pain lanced across Brand's face.

Rafe Bigelow's laugh boomed out across the dusty space that separated him from Brand.

'Don't you move, *Mister* Brand! Not one inch, else I'll cut you to the bone. You ever see what a good man can do with one of these? I have and I've done it too. Ain't a pretty thing to see. Like I say I'm good with this so you step easy around me.'

Brand needed no convincing. The man was good. He had already proved it. Brand's right arm burned with pain from shoulder to fingertip. Blood ran its length, dripping into the dust. The open gash across the back of his hand might have been done with a red-hot iron.

Bigelow's eyes flickered casually across the sprawled bodies of his former employees, and he said:

'You proved one thing. They weren't worth what I was payin' 'em.'

'Buy scum you can't expect anything better,'

91

Brand said. He spoke as a man who lived by the gun and had proved he was better because he was still alive, he was still around. Further proof of his skill was the fact that he had taken out Bigelow's three hired guns single handed. Not that he felt he needed to justify himself to Rafe Bigelow. Brand had never felt the need to brag about his ability to kill with an almost casual proficiency. Knowing it himself didn't always sit too comfortably on his shoulders, but it was a fact he had learned to live with.

'I don't suppose Yorrick or Hamner will be coming back either?' Bigelow enquired.

'If they do turn up we'll have one hell of a problem,' Brand said. 'What was the deal, Bigelow? Did they come cheaper the more you hired? Must have been a pretty bad barrel you were scraping.'

'Point taken,' Bigelow said. He smiled coldly. 'I'll take your advice next time I hire on. Check 'em for quality. Damn shame you're on the wrong side of the line.'

'Can't take the smell on your side,' Brand replied without thinking, and regretted it as Bigelow's hand sent the whip into motion again. The vicious lash made contact with Brand's body, coiling around his upper torso. Blood soaked through Brand's ripped shirt.

'Don't rile me any more than I already am,' Bigelow yelled. 'Damn you, Brand, you made a fool of me once. Ain't goin' to happen again. No way I'm lettin' you get near my goods, or Benito. Hell, I got me a damn good deal going on with that crazy Apache. He aims to keep fighting and he's getting

92

more bucks joining him all the time. And that white feller sidin' him pays good money to keep Benito in guns and whiskey.'

'Bigelow, don't be a damn fool. How long do you think Benito can last? He's got too much going against him. If I don't get him Crook will. He won't quit until he has Benito.'

Bigelow grinned. 'Think I ain't figured that? Long as it does last I'll keep supplying Benito.'

'*Not any longer!*'

The voice came from behind Bigelow. Brand recognized Niana. Her words were followed by the sound of a shot. Rafe Bigelow grunted and stepped forward, his face twisting with pain. He began to turn, seeking the source of the shot. Brand could see he still held the whip, and the thought of what it might do to Niana's lovely young body galvanized him into action. He remembered the rifle he had left leaning against the nearby wall. He went for it, taking long strides, and snatched it up. He aimed it at Bigelow's broad back. There was a spreading patch of blood soaking the man's shirt. It would take more than one bullet to stop a man with Bigelow's build.

'*Niana, get down,*' Brand yelled.

His warning made Bigelow stop. The big man began to turn towards Brand. He was already activating the long bullwhip again when Brand's first shot cracked out. He was holding the rifle at hip-level and he just kept firing and levering, over and over until the rifle was empty. Brass shell casings littered the ground at his feet. Smoke curled from the hot barrel.

Rafe Bigelow was down on the ground, on his back, staring up at the sun. The whip lay in his relaxed hand and bright blood was spattered across his ravaged chest. As Brand walked by him Bigelow's spilt blood, dark and thick, was already being sucked away by the parched earth beneath him.

Niana only looked at Bigelow once as she moved to meet Brand. She still held the Colt in her hand and when she became aware she hurriedly thrust it back into the holster on her hip.

'Are you hurt?' she asked.

Brand shrugged.

'Not as bad as I might have been if you hadn't jumped in. I ought to be damned mad at you. I told you to stay back. Aren't Apache women supposed to do as they're told?'

Niana's eyes flashed angrily.

'That is true. But you are teaching me the way of the *Pinda Lickoyi* and I have heard your women do not always obey their men.'

Brand scowled.

'You believe that? Then I'm teaching you the wrong things.'

Niana smiled.

'Not everything you teach me is bad, Brand.'

He growled in disgust and grabbed her arm, leading her back to the store. He took her through to Bigelow's office. He put down his rifle, leaned his weight against Bigelow's desk and tipped it over. Concealed beneath the desk was a wooden trapdoor. Brand hooked a finger through the hole provided and raised the door. A rush of stale, dry air rose to meet him. A wooden ladder led down to the darkness of the cellar.

'Is this where the guns are kept?' Niana asked.

'I reckon so.'

'What are you going to do?'

Brand kicked the trapdoor shut.

'Get cleaned up. Find a better shirt than the one I'm wearing. Then get something to eat.'

'But the guns . . .'

'They're not liable to wander off and Bigelow's men seem to have lost interest. We'll deal with the guns before we go.'

He took her through to the store again.

'Be a shame not to stock up on a few items before we leave.'

'Would you object, *señor*, if we also indulged in the opportunity that has presented itself?'

Brand glanced at the thin-faced Mexican standing in the doorway. He wore dusty white pants and shirt and clutched a tattered straw hat in nervous brown hands. His feet were bare. He looked half-starved. Over his shoulder Brand could see more brown faces, dark eyes full of anticipation. *Why not*, he thought. Bigelow had probably been using these people for years, making them pay heavily for anything they needed.

'Help yourselves,' he said. 'Take what you need.'

He watched them rush by, scattering as they ran into the store. At least some good would come from all the death that had visited this place. He had killed four men. A high price to pay, even to fill the empty bellies of starving Mexicans.

CHAPTER 9

The Rio Bavispa lay behind and below them as they rode up into the rocky foothills of the Sierra Madre. They followed no marked trail, but there was no hesitation in Niana's line of travel. She knew where they were heading and Brand allowed her to get on with the task. For his part he kept a watchful eye open for sign of others in the area. This was no time to run into a patrol of the *Rurales,* or a band of Mexican *banditos,* let alone any stray Apaches. Brand concentrated on what lay ahead.

They had stayed over at Bigelow's long enough to rest and replenish their supplies. The Mexicans who lived around the trading post had shown their gratitude for what Brand had done by throwing an impromptu fiesta. They were a sorry collection of peasants simply trying to scratch a living of sorts from the barren land. Bigelow had forced them deeper into debt by allowing them credit and then charging the kind of prices that kept them permanently under his thumb. They had remained that way until Brand's action had freed them.

Niana, with her Apache logic, had not been able to grasp why they had not fought back against Bigelow. She could not understand the way of the Mexicans. Brand had done his best to explain the Mexican mentality. He failed to convince her and they talked late into the night, as she tended his wounds with some Apache salve she had made from gathered herbs. They were sharing a hut the Mexicans had allowed them to use. Brand did his best to stop Niana's chatter as she complained about the Mexicans. Everything failed until he did the one thing that he knew would silence her. He kissed her, and she responded with her usual enthusiasm. It was a long time before they both fell asleep through sheer exhaustion.

The following morning Niana stocked up their supplies from Bigelow's shelves while Brand went into the cellar beneath the office. He found exactly what he had expected. Rifles, boxes of ammunition. Wooden casks holding whiskey. There were even barrels of black powder and lead blocks for bullet-making. He took a supply of ammunition for his own use.

The Mexicans had pretty well stripped the store of its contents. Brand found a couple of large cans of coal-oil. He opened them and poured the contents of one down into the cellar. The second one he splashed around the store itself. Standing at the door he lit a match and touched it to an oil-soaked rag, tossing it on to the oily floor of the store. He watched the flames start to spread through the interior, then went outside.

A group of the Mexicans had gathered to watch and Brand was forced to yell for them to move away. Within minutes the store was a mass of flame. Smoke rose in a thick column, staining the blue sky. Eventually the fire penetrated the cellar and generated enough heat to set off the black powder. There was a muffled explosion that created enough power to blow the store building apart. Debris was hurled in all directions.

The Mexicans raised a yell, grinning wildly as they watched.

Once it was over there was nothing to keep Brand. He and Niana mounted up, took their farewell of the Mexicans, and rode out. They cut off to the south, for the border and Sonora, looking for Nante's secret trail that led into the Sierra Madre.

Niana reined in her pony and waited until Brand was beside her. She raised an arm and indicated the high peaks towering over them.

'That is where we go,' she said. 'The place is far into the heart of the mountains.'

Brand took a look around. Nante had chosen well. It *was* rough country. He expected it to get rougher as they pushed deeper in. He was right. The way became steeper, the ground underfoot treacherous. He saw the wisdom of using Apache ponies. They were well suited to negotiating this formidable terrain. Even so they had to dismount on more than one occasion and lead the animals across some difficult stretch of mountain slope.

They camped that night in a ravine that had been

formed long ago by the splitting of a vast bed of solid rock. It had left behind a jagged, wide crack with walls that rose close on a hundred feet high. Brand built a small fire beneath a rock overhang; the curve of stone above the fire kept the flames from being reflected in the dark night sky.

'As I have learned your ways,' Niana said, 'so you have seen the way of the Apache.'

'If a man wants to grow old out here, he learns fast,' Brand said.

'Will you grow old, Brand? Or will you die soon because of the gun you wear?'

He took a moment to consider that. It was a question he could not rightly answer. Thinking about it made him realize the future was something he seldom considered in any depth. He lived from day to day, almost from moment to moment. There never seemed much advantage in looking too far ahead. Nor did he think towards the time when he might be an old man, too slow and frail to be useful at what he was doing now. The thought of being old and feeble did not appeal. Maybe the best thing would be for him to die sometime while he still had a chance to decide how he might go. He didn't relish the thought of having to be put out to pasture. When the time came he wanted it to be quick.

When he became aware of his train of thought Brand mentally shook himself. He had enough to think about in the present. The future could look after itself.

He spooned beans out of the pan on to plates, adding strips of crisped bacon. He passed Niana her plate, then sat back with his own. Glancing across at the Apache girl he wondered if she was still waiting for an answer.

'We all have to die some day,' he said. 'Nobody knows when his time's coming, so all he can do is live the most each day brings and lie down when his time comes.'

Niana raised her head and studied him gravely.

'Many times when you speak it is like listening to Nante. I think you were much alike in what you thought.'

'Nante was a warrior I respected. No shame in being compared to someone like him.'

They finished their meal and cleaned away the utensils. Brand sat with a mug of coffee, watching Niana tend the ponies and make sure they were well tethered. Later she came to him, slipping naked beneath his blanket. The night was soft dark around them, peaceful and quiet, and they saw no reason to disturb that quiet with words.

CHAPTER 10

Mid-morning of the next day found them well into the timberline. The undulating and rocky canyon country lay beneath a wide-spread forest of pine and oak. They rode through places where the trees grew so thickly they blocked out the sun. It was a silent, twilight place, the leaf mold damp and thick on the ground. Without warning they would break free and find themselves riding across open ground, or fording a swift-flowing stream that came tumbling and foaming down out of the high places. It was beautiful, savage country, barely touched by man, and retained much of its primeval atmosphere from thousands of years ago.

It took most of the day before they left the timber far behind and came out on an open, bare rocky slope of the mountain. They were high up now, with the ever-present peaks looming close. The sun blazed down on them, bouncing from the bleached rock, and dust rose from beneath the hoofs of the ponies, thick and sour-tasting. It stung their eyes, leaving them itchy and red-rimmed.

Late in the afternoon Niana led them to a sheltered basin where a clear spring bubbled fiercely from a fissure in the rocks, filling the shallow rock *tinaja* formed by the constant, wearing flow of water.

The first thing Brand did was to empty the warm water from their water skins, then refill them with the fresh cold spring water. Then he kept watch as Niana knelt by the pool and rinsed her burning, dusty face. She opened her shirt and scooped handfuls of the cool water over her body. When she had done she took a small drink.

'Give me the rifle,' she said. 'I will watch now.'

Brand handed her the weapon and went to the pool. His ritual followed Niana's almost identically. The water, when he took a drink, was cold and fresh and for a moment he found himself wondering how far it had travelled beneath the mountain before emerging into the daylight.

'In the morning we will reach the place,' Niana said when he rejoined her.

'You want to make camp here?' Brand asked.

She shook her head. Handing him the rifle she pointed up the mountain.

'We go higher. There will be a better place. We have plenty of time before darkness.'

He nodded, aware that he was staring at her in a way that had nothing to do with why they were here. He was letting himself become attached to this healthy and desirable young woman. He drew his mind back to the present, angry because once again he was letting his desire for her cloud his judgement. It wasn't the first time it had happened and he knew it wouldn't be the last. The fairer sex had a hold over him that he often fought against and usually lost.

He followed Niana back to where the ponies were standing. They took them to the pool and let them slake their thirst and rest for a while. When they remounted and moved off, with Niana in the lead, Brand found he was watching the way her firm, rounded buttocks rolled with the pony's motion.

What the hell, he thought. *Come the day when he didn't notice something like that he would start to worry fast. Maybe his destiny was to end up a dirty old man.*

Just before dark Niana brought them to a place deep inside a jumble of shattered rock at the base of a towering cliff. Brand noticed the marks of old fires.

'This was a place Nante used often. If he needed to be alone he would come here.'

Niana slid from her pony and led it further into the rocks. Brand followed and saw there was a small stand of trees, a shallow stream. Even a little grass. They saw to the ponies, then hauled their gear back to where Niana was able to start a small fire.

'If you live with the Earth and not against it, then it will always provide,' she said as she prepared their meal.

'Well, you haven't been wrong yet. Nante taught you well. He would have been proud of you.'

'And are you proud for me too, Brand?' she asked. 'As your woman?'

He glanced across the flames at her. She was studying him with an earnest expression in her eyes.

'No man could ask for better,' he said, and found he meant every word.

She nodded in satisfaction and went back to her cooking, leaving Brand to ponder on his rash words.

While they ate he asked her about the hideout. Niana pointed to the high rim of the cliff.

'On the far side of that place is where Benito hides. In the rocks are houses, built by the Indians of Mexico a long time ago. Nante told me they were here even before the Spanish came.'

'What about the way in?'

'There is only one. A trail. It goes up the side of the great cliff. Narrow even for a pony. One at a time only. A man alone can defend the entrance, and there will always be someone watching.'

Filling his mug with hot coffee Brand stared up the sheer cliff face. If he couldn't get in by the front door then he would have to find another route, and from what Niana had been saying that other route would be up the damn cliff. The thought didn't sit well – but he accepted he wasn't going to get in by any other way.

Niana seemed to sense his mood. She moved close beside him, reaching out to touch his face.

'What troubles Brand?'

He pointed towards the distant cliff.

'Come morning I'm going to climb that damn thing.' He smiled. 'That is what troubles Brand.'

'Can it be done?'

'We'll know soon enough.'

She leaned her warm young body against his. Kissing him with her customary hunger.

'Then tonight you should rest well.'

'If you say so.'

106

'But not yet,' she added, smiling gently as she began to shed her clothing.

Her warmth stirred him and he pulled her close. Niana stared into his eyes. What was it that aroused her so much each time she touched him? She recalled their first meeting outside Nante's hut, remembering that she had not liked him then. Yet now his very touch made her yearn for him, her body reacting strongly to his demands.

They made love with a passion. She found her need for him was tinged with desperation, because she could not forget he would be leaving her in the morning. Then he would go looking for Benito, and though his skills would be a match for Benito's warriors she knew he was not invincible. He could die as easily as any man.

As she lay beside him, the warmth of their coupling still strong, she traced the line of the scars that marked his naked body. He was one who lived with violence, existed in a world that had little time for pleasure or peace. Brand had accepted his role, living for the moment, and taking what he could from each snatched fragment of time. She felt him stir against her and she drew him closer. She did not want him to go, but she would have no say in the matter. Once his path had been chosen he followed it faithfully. There was no turning back. He would stay with his decision, never accepting the thought of defeat. It was a mark of his pride that he stayed the course. A man like Brand had that and maybe nothing else. It marked him as different from other men, placing him apart. A lonely place to be but for Brand the only place. In that respect he was like the Apache. A warrior was only a warrior as long as he kept face. If he lost that he was nothing.

Niana lifted her head and gazed over his naked shoulder. The dark rise of the great cliff rose in the distance. It seemed to have a life of its own, a brooding, seemingly invincible enemy. And an enemy that might claim his life so easily. A moment of dread filled her mind.

What could he do – one man – against Benito and his warriors?

Only at this moment did she consider that coming here alone had been a mistake. Crook and Sieber had been wrong in allowing one man to take on a mission that needed the strength of many. It was not fair that he should be expected to face Benito alone. Yet even as the thought passed through her mind, she knew there was nothing she could do to change things. Nor could she even speak of her fears. No matter how she felt, those thoughts would stay within her. It was not for a woman to interfere in the ways of a man, no matter how she felt about him. That was the Apache way, and Niana was enough of a woman to know her place. She lay against him, holding him tightly, wondering if this would be the last time they would be together.

CHAPTER 11

'Stay here as long as it's safe,' Brand said. 'No telling how long I might be gone. I don't want you hanging on if things start to go wrong.' He glanced up from reloading the big Colt he had just cleaned and checked. 'Promise, Niana. I don't want you sitting here until it snows. If you have to leave tie my pony so he can't run. I might just make it back.'

'Do not speak so, Brand. You will come back. I feel it in my heart.'

'Well, you go right on feeling that way. It might just bring me some luck.'

Brand holstered the Colt, slipping the hammer loop into place. He didn't want to risk the chance of the gun slipping out of the holster while he was scaling the cliff. He picked up his mug and drained it. The sun was well up and it was time he started out. There was no telling how long it was going to take him to make the climb.

He got to his feet and went to Niana, kissed her, then turned away and moved out of the rocks. It was a good quarter-mile to the base of the cliff. He recalled Niana telling him that Benito kept a constant guard at the top of the trail leading into the hideout. He stayed under cover as best he was able, lucky that the terrain was rough, full of fissures choked with brush, scattered boulders and trees. It took him more than an hour to reach the base of the cliff.

He leaned against a handy slab of rock and stared up at the towering cliff. *What the hell had he let himself in for?* Up close the rock face was not as sheer and smooth as distance had made it appear. Even so it did look a great deal higher from where he stood. He was glad now that he hadn't bothered to bring along anything liable to interfere with his climbing. He took his time picking a place to start. A few hundred yards along he found what he was looking for.

A wide fissure in the face of the cliff. It was a great crack that snaked its way up the towering wall of rock. At the foot of the cliff lay a jumble of tumbled rock and debris that had spilled from the fissure at the time of its creation. Brand studied it for a time. It looked to be the best chance he was going to get.

He clambered over the pile of rocks at the base and moved into the shadow of the fissure. The first part of the climb would be comparatively easy as the lower section of the fissure was composed of a long, steep slope.

He was staring up the weathered rock, his mind absently acknowledging the utter silence of the place, when his ears caught the merest whisper of sound off to his left. Brand's eyes moved in that direction quicker than his body, and he caught a fleeting glimpse of a darting shadow lunging at him. Then he turned, meeting head on the half-naked figure of a leaping Apache. He reached for the wrist of the hand holding a thick-bladed knife.

The Apache's stocky body slammed into him and they crashed to the ground. The Apache's free hand clawed at Brand's throat, fingers digging into his flesh. Brand knew he couldn't hold off the knife and deal with the hand around his throat at the same time. He swung up his legs, scissoring his thighs around the Apache's body, squeezing hard against the man's ribs. He felt his hand slipping on the Apache's sweating flesh, saw the knife starting to drop towards his chest. He put all he had into the grip he had around the Apache's body and was rewarded with a the crack of bone.

The Apache grunted in pain as ribs caved in. His grip on Brand's throat slackened a little. Brand slashed his left hand across his body, knocking the Apache's hand from his throat, then drove it back, hand bunched into a hard fist. He felt the Apache's mouth cave in under the blow. Hot blood sprayed from split lips. Brand reached across and closed his fingers around the wrist of the knife hand. Then he arched his whole body and rolled the Apache off him.

The Apache reacted quickly, letting his body slide away, getting his feet under him. Brand hung on to the wrist and let the Apache haul him upright. The moment he regained his feet he lashed out with his left foot, the toe of his boot driving up between the

Apache's thighs. The Apache's mouth opened in a silent scream of pain, his legs buckling. Brand stepped in close, twisting the Apache's wrist.

He kept on twisting even after he felt resistance. Bone snapped and the Apache dropped the knife. Brand bent to snatch it up and drove a shoulder into the Indian's chest, slamming him back against the rocks. As he began to straighten the Apache launched himself off the rock, still full of fight despite his injuries. It was no effort on Brand's part to push the knife forward and let the Apache impale himself on his own blade. The knife went in up to the hilt, a spurt of warm blood covering Brand's hand. He let go of the knife and the Apache curled up at his feet.

Brand slumped back and sat against a chunk of rock. He was sweating, his chest heaving from the exertion of the struggle. He ached in a number of places. He saw that the Apache had stopped moving now.

Where the hell had this one come from? And were there more in the area?

He took a quick look round and found an answer to his question.

In the shade of some rocks close by he found the Apache's gear. There was also the skinned carcass of a deer. The Apache had been out hunting and had spotted Brand. He realized how close it had been. If he hadn't picked up the faint sound of the buck's approach . . . Brand corrected himself; there was no point in worrying over what might have been. What did matter was his survival.

112

He collected the Apache's belongings and hid them down a deep crevice in the rock, along with the deer carcass. He moved the body and pushed it into the crevice too. Then he tumbled some loose rock on top to hide the evidence. There was no telling how soon the Apache might be missed. If others came looking for him it was going to make Brand's approach to the hideout that much harder. If they did show they would find him – Brand didn't fool himself on that score. Good as he was the Apache were the masters. Hiding the body might allow him some extra time, and that was something he needed if he was going to scale that damned cliff. It was a pity about the blood spilled on the rocks, but there was nothing he could do about that.

Time was against him now. Brand started his climb, working his way up the first section of the slope, moving as fast as he dared, yet he was having to pause more than once while he figured out his next move. There was no way he could achieve the climb in a straight line. The mass of rock was composed of varied shapes and sizes, some as big as houses, and he had to move around these before he could carry on with his ascent.

He had to quit worrying about how he was doing timewise. He simply concentrated on climbing. Moving upwards, knowing too that he had a hell of a way to go, and this was the easy part.

It began to get warm. The sun penetrated the fissure and the heat began to build. Sweat poured off Brand. His shirt clung to his back, sodden with his sweat. His limbs ached. He wasn't used to this kind of exertion. He was putting strain on muscles he seldom used in his normal life. His narrow-toed, high-heeled boots didn't make things any easier. They had been designed to keep a man's foot in his stirrup, not for climbing mountains. After a time Brand quit thinking about the reasons he shouldn't be doing this and concentrated on just climbing.

He reached the place where the initial slope tapered off and found himself faced by a scarred, fissured rock face that, while not vertical, wasn't far off it. He leaned his back against the hot rock and studied the way ahead, or, to be exact, *above*. He figured he had to have been a little crazy to have chosen this way into Benito's hideout. As he sleeved sweat from his face he caught sight of his hand, it was scratched and bloody. So was his other hand. Brand grunted with annoyance. He pushed away from the rock and reached for the first handhold.

Now he simply climbed, looking neither up nor down. He put all he had into moving slowly up the rock face, his concentration on the next hand or foothold.

He was no more than a tiny speck on that sun-bleached spread of rock, albeit a living thing with only a single thought in his mind – to reach the top. He ignored the heat and the sweat, the bloody flesh of his hands and even the throbbing ache in every muscle he possessed. He had only one worry. A single, nagging thought that centered on Niana. He was worried about her and hoped she was all right.

A knob of rock gave way under one boot. He felt his body fall away from the rock face and he was sure he was going to fall. But then his right hand snatched at a thin ledge of rock, fingers clamping tight to the projection. His arm muscles begged for relief as he hung suspended by one hand. It seemed an eternity before he was able to regain his former hold and he refused to move for some time. He was trembling violently, stomach churning. Sweat ran down into his eyes, stinging.

He began to climb again. Slowly. He became aware of a stinging sensation down one side of his face and realized he must have banged it when he slipped. The pain was something to concentrate on – and at first he failed to notice the rock face starting to curve away from him. When he did he realized that he was nearing the top. The fact failed to impress him. He was close to exhaustion. When the rock eventually became level beneath him he crawled on his stomach, away from the sheer drop.

He sought out a shallow crevice, out of the sun's glare and also away from unfriendly eyes. He had reached the top and for now that had to be enough. He needed to rest. He was in no fit state to face anyone at the moment, let alone someone like Benito and his band of Apaches – or the mystery white man. They were all going to have to wait a little longer.

CHAPTER 12

Brand slept fitfully through the rest of the day, not daring to let himself go too deeply under. He needed to rest but at the same time he had to stay reasonably alert to be aware of any potential danger. He decided to move once it was dark. He had no idea yet what he was up against and figured that darkness would at least give him a degree of cover while he assessed the odds.

The sun set slowly, gradually sinking out of sight in a flaring spread of dying light that seemed to set the land on fire. A violent setting for a violent land. Brand eased himself stiffly out of cover, stretching his aching body, then moved off along the wide, rocky rim of the basin that concealed Benito's camp. Glancing over the inner edge of the rim he saw that the sides of the basin curved downwards in a series of long slopes; a lot easier way to get down than the way he had come up.

There was a time before the moon rose when he found himself moving in almost total darkness. Below him, across the basin, nestled against the lower slopes of the far side, he saw the old Indian rock houses, illuminated by a number of glowing fires, the weathered stone softened by the flickering orange flames. He saw, too, that many of the window slots showed light: oil-lamps throwing yellow beams into the outer darkness.

Brand began to move down the inner slopes. His progress was hampered by the fact that the slopes held numerous stretches of loose shale. These he had to move around, not daring to cross them in case he started a slide. The sound of moving shale would carry far in the night silence.

The moon rose almost in the same instant that Brand reached the basin floor. It flooded the area with its pale, bluish light. Brand dropped behind the closest cover and stayed there, the night air cooling the sweat on his face. He took out the Colt, gripping the butt firmly and feeling better for having it in his hand.

Yard by yard Brand crossed the wide basin, moving himself closer to the Apache campsite with every step. He could hear sounds now; voices of men and women; the restless sound of corralled horses and ponies. Mingled smells reached his nostrils too; wood-smoke; the drifting aroma of cooked meat. Brand felt his stomach rebel against the lack of food.

And then he was close enough to be able to see everything he needed. He crossed a shallow stream of cold, clear water, and burrowed deep into a clump of thick brush on the far bank. Directly across from where he crouched the lighted windows and doorways of the old Indian dwellings beckoned. Below them on the flat earth were the cookfires around which he could make out the figures of the Apache women busy with their chores. To the right of him was the large corral, holding a good-sized herd of horses and ponies. Close by the corral he spotted a couple of freight wagons – evidence of the presence of whites. The way off to his left would be the way out, leading to the narrow trail by which the Apaches came and went. He recalled Niana telling him how narrow that trail was. If that were so, whoever had brought in the wagons certainly knew their business.

Brands studied the dwellings. If Benito was here, which would be his resting place? There would be no trouble recognizing Benito. The Apache's face was well known to Brand from the times their paths had crossed. Benito would be older now, but Brand would know him – and he also knew what he was going to have to do. Talking to a man like Benito was simply a waste of time and energy. The Apache had gone beyond reason. His treatment of Nante had proved that. Benito had to be removed, without thought. With no conscious hesitation.

In a word, Benito had to be *killed*.

And what about this white renegade? Brand hadn't given him much thought. But the time was fast approaching when he would have to acknowledge the man's existence. The renegade posed as much of a threat as Benito did. Brand had little feeling for a man who openly encouraged the deaths of his own kind, urging the Apaches on to make their bloody killing sprees again and again. He tried to understand why a man would do such a thing. It was beyond him for the moment. Perhaps the renegade was as crazy as Benito. Two madmen for the price of one.

It came to Brand that *he* was not doing this for any price.

He was doing it because a dying old man had asked him. Nante, his friend, whom Brand had been unable to refuse. He had at first thought it was out of loyalty but now he wasn't so sure. He'd been craving to get back into action back at Sarita's place. He had been too long away from it. His restless inactivity had been challenged on this assignment. Brand had wanted action – and he was getting it.

He heard a rustle of sound. A dark figure approached the stream. A young Apache girl was carrying a clay pot. She crouched beside the stream and filled the pot. She was no more than ten feet from where Brand hid. He watched her closely, seeking any sign that she might be aware of his presence. The girl lifted the dripping pot and turned back to the main camp, her sturdy body moving freely under the thin buckskin dress she wore.

The sight of the dripping clay pot reminded him how thirsty he was and he turned to bend over the stream, scooping water to his lips. As he straightened he heard someone else approaching. Not an Apache. He was hearing the rap of hard-soled leather boots, not soft moccasins. He eased back into the brush, picking out the slim shape moving his way. He lifted the Colt, but the figure moved on by and paused at the edge of the stream.

The newcomer was a woman. A white woman too.

Maybe a prisoner? He doubted that. She was moving around too freely. The only other explanation was that she was with the white renegade. Brand saw an opportunity presenting itself. He waited a while longer to see what the woman was doing and saw her strip off the thin white blouse she was wearing. As she knelt at the stream's edge, scooping up cool water to wash herself, moonlight gleamed against her white skin, outlining the full shape of her dark-tipped breasts. *It seemed a shame to disturb her,* Brand thought wryly as he moved to close in on her. The woman had chosen a spot where the brush screened her from the camp, and Brand was grateful for that. It would conceal him as well. He came up behind her as she stood up, letting the warmth of the night air dry her. Her hands were reaching for the buttons of her dark skirt when Brand let the muzzle of the Colt touch her naked back.

'Don't bother, lady, you haven't the time,' he said firmly.

He heard her involuntary gasp, the sound forming into a single word as she turned to face him.

'*Brand!*'

He found himself staring into the face of Lucilla St Clair. For a moment he thought his eyes were playing tricks on him. She had cropped her long blonde hair down to a boyish cut that clung softly to the contours of her head. The face was the same. Bright, exciting eyes, full, soft lips curving now into a pouting smile. Now she faced him he recalled the ripe, full breasts and for a moment he was back on that train, in her private compartment, with Lucilla standing naked before him, offering herself to him. He hadn't taken up her offer then. He doubted if she would make the same mistake again.

He raised the Colt and levelled it at her lovely face.

'Don't be fooled,' he said. 'I'll use this if I have to. If you don't believe me, Lucilla, you just go ahead and let out that yell you're working up to.'

She stared at him, anger making her features hard, but she knew he was not one to make idle threats.

'Do you mind if I get dressed? Or do you need longer?'

Brand couldn't help grinning, his teeth white against his dark face.

'Seems to me the last time we were in this position you couldn't wait to get your clothes off.'

'*You bastard*!' she spat. 'But I suppose we all make mistakes.'

'Yes, ma'am.'

The words came out automatically. Brand was doing some quick thinking. If Lucilla was here it was more than likely he would run into another old acquaintance. The last time he'd seen him was when they had been fighting over Brand's attempt to stop Beauregard St Clair from assassinating President Cleveland.

'So how is Mr Royce?' he asked.

Lucilla glanced up from buttoning her blouse, her eyes flashing with unconcealed rage.

'He'll be pleased to see you, Brand. And even more pleased when he gets to kill you.'

Brand believed her. There was enough venom in

her tone to have dropped him in his tracks if words had been able to kill. He figured she must have hated him badly. Not only had he destroyed her father's organization, killing him in the process, but Brand had made it impossible for her to return to the great St Clair mansion and its adjoining estates. He had utterly changed her life.

'I don't aim to give him the chance,' Brand said. 'That murdering son of a bitch has got as long to live as it takes me to find him. I made the mistake of letting him get away alive last time. Because of that he was able to work up this unholy mess. Seems fitting I should put him out of his misery.'

'You haven't a chance, Brand. You managed to get in here but you won't get out. Once Benito finds you're here there'll be twenty Apaches gunning for you. Plus Parker and me.'

'Such talk from a Southern belle,' Brand said softly, and then he slapped her across the face with his open left hand, hard enough to make her head rock. 'Understand me, Lucilla. If I didn't actually need you right this minute I'd like as not be cutting that pretty white throat. But I do need you for a while, and you had better listen hard and do what I say first time round. A forty-five caliber bullet would make a hell of a mess of that face.'

He let the words sink in. He wanted Lucilla to realize he was in earnest over what he had said – which he was.

'What do you want from me?'

'Show me where the weapons are stored. Then I want to see Benito and Parker. He got any help?'

'Six hired guns.'

'I'm one of them for now. Understand?'

She nodded. 'What if we run into them?'

'You just show me where those damn guns are stored. I'll do the worrying for the both of us. Don't do anything silly, Lucilla. You might just walk away alive if you play your cards right.'

Her face turned ugly as she drew on the memories of their last confrontation.

'Did you give my father the same choice before you killed him?'

'As much of a chance as Sarah got.' His words were cold and devoid of emotion. Inside he was reliving the way Sarah Debenham had died and the fact that he had been unable to prevent her death. There was a fraction of a second when his control almost slipped. The Colt jerked in his hand as his fingers tightened around the butt and he could have pulled the trigger just as easily.

Lucilla saw the madness in his eyes. She realized the frailty of her position and she reacted out of instinct. She took a step back, her hands thrown up as if to ward off some unseen blow.

'Jason, no! For God's sake don't!'

Her protest snapped him out of his mood and he moved towards her. Even though he lowered his gun Lucilla saw his move as a continuation of the threat. She opened her mouth to scream and Brand knew there was no way she was going to help him now. As far as she was concerned he was going to hurt her, maybe even kill her, and her thoughts were directed towards her own survival. Before she could utter a sound Brand hit her, clipping her alongside one smooth brow with the barrel of the Colt. She fell away from him, body limp, half-sliding into the stream before he reached her. As he dragged her deeper into the brush Brand tore angrily at her skirt until he had enough material to tie her hands behind her back, tether her ankles and gag her.

He peered through the brush, searching the camp layout. How was he going to find the arms cache now? He knew the answer before his mind had fully compiled the question. He would do what he had done so many times before, and would probably do again . . . providing he was still alive.

He stretched out in the densest part of the brush and just studied what was going on in the camp. His gaze moved from left to right, seeking to pick out any detail that might provide him with the information he wanted.

Behind him Lucilla stirred. Brand didn't worry. She wasn't going anywhere, or raising any alarm. He'd tied and gagged her tighly enough to keep her from bothering him. But that situation might change at any moment. There was going to come a time when Lucia's absence became apparent. When that happened Brand didn't want to be sitting around doing nothing.

He focused his attention on the spot where the two freight wagons stood. Maybe the weapons were nearby, maybe still inside the wagons. It was a slim chance but worth investigating. He had nothing else to go on and had to start somewhere.

Easing out of the brush he crouched low and

waded into the stream. Its meandering course took it down beyond the corral and the parked wagons. Though the brush edging the stream didn't offer a continuous line of cover there was enough to give him a good chance to move undetected. He moved slowly, pausing often when shadowy figures passed close to the stream. His luck held. There were no more visits to the stream by any of the camp's occupiers.

By the time he drew level with the corral, close in near the rising wall of rock where the Indian dwellings had been carved out, Brand was sweating and it wasn't from the chill that was starting to drive away the lingering heat of day. He paused to wipe the sweat from his gunhand and moved out of the water. He crouched beside a thick corral corner post. Away from the lights coming from the rock dwellings and the camp-fires, this area was bathed in deep shadows.

The wagons were on the far side of the corral and Brand worked his way around to them. He moved slowly, not wanting to disturb the milling horse and pony herds penned inside the corral. It wouldn't take much to alarm them. The last thing he wanted was a whole herd setting up a racket.

When he reached the first wagon Brand checked beneath the canvas that was draped over the sides. It was empty and so was the second wagon when he had a look in that one. Brand peered beyond the wagons in the direction of the rock face and the houses cut from it. Maybe the weapons were in there.

He stepped around the end of the wagon and came to a dead stop, face to face with a lean figure

126

wearing grubby Levis and a flannel shirt.

One of Royce's men?

'That you, Sam?' the man asked, stepping forward. A match flared as the man struck it against the iron rim of one of the wagon wheels. He raised the match to light the thin cigar dangling from a corner of his mouth. In the brief glare of the match he saw Brand's face. 'Hey! You ain't Sam. . . .'

Brand lunged forward. His left hand grabbed the man's shirtfront, yanking him off balance, swinging him round and slamming him against the side of the wagon. The back of the man's skull rapped sharply into contact with the hard wood, the cigar jumping from his lips. Brand rammed the muzzle of his Colt against the side of the man's face, letting him hear the hammer click back.

'You get one chance, friend,' he said quickly. 'Your choice. Either stay alive, or die.'

In the semi-light the man's eyes gleamed in panic. Brand could almost smell the fear oozing from every pore.

'Hell, mister, keep ahold on to that damn hammer.'

Brand pressed harder into soft flesh.

'Friend, I've got a weak thumb, so don't take too long.'

'*Easy*! Jesus Christ, easy.' The man was visibly scared. 'What the hell is it you want?'

'Where are the guns stored?'

The man jerked a thumb in the direction of the rock dwellings.

'In there. Behind those wooden doors.'

Brand had the information he needed. He slipped

the man's revolver from his holster.

'You got any more matches?' he asked.

The man frowned, then nodded. He fumbled in his shirt pocket and produced four wooden matches. Brand pocketed them.

'Grateful, friend,' Brand said, then slammed the barrel of his Colt across the side of the man's skull. The man stumbled to his knees and Brand hit him twice more before he went flat out.

Brand reached the place where the weapons were kept without meeting anyone else. The newly rigged wooden doors opened easily and without any sound on their leather hinges. Brand slipped inside and took a quick look round. It was becoming a familiar sight. The stacked cases of rifles. Boxes of ammunition and casks of black powder. It had been the same at Bigelow's, and at the cache of arms Beauregard St. Clair had concealed in the swamps bordering his estate. Brand didn't waste time. He followed the same procedure as previously. He broke open a couple of casks of black powder and spread the contents of one over the remaining casks. He used the second cask to lay a thick trail of powder back outside, tossing the cask back through the door.

He had a match in his fingers when a thought came to him. He turned and made his way back to the corral, dropping the bar gate. He moved to the rear of the milling animals, took out his Colt and triggered a couple of shots. The horses and ponies burst free from the confines of the corral, spreading as they cleared the gate. Dust boiled up in thick clouds and the thunder of hoofs mingled with the shrill sounds of frightened animals. The free animals began to drive towards the main camp.

Brand returned to his black powder. He struck a match and as it flared he dropped it on to the heap of powder he'd built up at the end of his trail. The powder hissed and crackled. It flared suddenly, a tongue of fire that began to snake its way towards the entrance to the weapons store. The moment the powder ignited Brand turned and ran back for the empty corral, throwing himself down on the ground.

The flame vanished into the store. Silence followed and remained. Brand swore, wondering if his trick was going to work this time. It had always been effective before. He raised his head and stared at the dark entrance to the store.

The explosion made the ground beneath him shake. The interior of the store was abruptly filled with flame and smoke. As the force of the explosion spread outwards, through the entrance, there was a rush of hot wind, debris and dust filling the air. That was followed by a fierce gout of flame. It reached out, writhing and twisting, and set alight the closest of the wagons. The heat reached as far as the corral, stinging Brand's flesh as he rolled away, scrambling to his feet as the flame died.

He could hear men shouting from the general direction of the campsite. Horse and ponies were still chasing around in every direction. Brand couldn't see much due to the swirling clouds of dust, but he knew as sure as he was standing on his own two feet that he was going to have visitors any second.

A figure materialized from the dust. A white man. Broad and long-haired. He was naked to the waist and carried a revolver in his left hand. As he emerged from the dust his attention was caught by the tall, dark figure standing by the corral and he knew he was facing a stranger. The man didn't hesitate. He kept coming forward, raising his gun and sending a shot towards Brand.

The heavy bullet clipped Brand's left side, drawing blood. Brand's reaction was automatic. He triggered a pair of shots at the man, stopping him in his tracks for a split second before the impact of the .45s kicked him back off his feet. He went into the dirt and stayed there. Brand made his way towards the stream. He was fully committed now and there was only one way out of the mess he'd started. He had to get to Benito and Parker Royce. If he could deal with them he might still walk away from this place.

He hit the water and moved upstream, making for the place where he had left Lucilla. There was still a great deal of confusion. Voices yelling. Asking questions – some angry, others just confused. In the background he could hear the horses and ponies. As he neared where he had left Lucilla a wild-eyed horse broke through the brush and splashed across the stream into the darkness beyond.

Brand saw that Lucilla had gone the moment he stepped out of the water. She could not have freed herself so it meant someone had found her. By now Royce would know Brand was in the camp somewhere. And so would Benito.

Damn!

Lucilla had been right – any minute now he would have the whole bunch of them after him.

He took out the Colt he'd acquired earlier, and with a gun in each hand he eased into the thick brush. A nervous knot of horses were milling around just beyond the brush. In the center of the camp most of the cookfires had been stamped down, leaving spirals of smoke to drift around the area. Brand saw there weren't many people about. They would have gathered at the explosion site, but once his presence had been acknowledged they would all start to move back, searching.

He slipped out of the brush, skirting the bunched horses, and crossed the open ground until he was able to hug the stone wall beneath the rock dwellings. Carved steps led up to the various levels, stone galleries running along the front of each row of dwellings.

He went up the first set of steps. Somewhere up ahead he needed to find himself a place to hide. Benito's band of Apaches would be scouring the area in a short time. Brand wanted to be hidden by then. He just hoped that his luck held and they didn't guess he had remained close to home. He was counting on them figuring he was somewhere out in the darkness – away from the camp – not in its very center.

CHAPTER 13

Bright sunlight shone directly into Brand's eyes. He turned away from the glare, easing his stiffened body. He was sluggish with sleep, realizing he had rested longer than he'd intended. As his senses cleared he became aware of activity below him. He crawled to the edge of the broad ledge and looked down on the Apache camp.

A group of mounted, armed Apaches were engaged in an agitated conversation with a single Apache who stood his ground before them. Even from his perch high above the camp Brand recognized the man he had come to find.

Benito.

And he also knew the tall man standing nearby. It was Parker Royce. His hired guns stood a little way off, looking more than a little nervous in the face of the restless Apaches. Watching them Brand wished he had a good rifle in his hands. The range was too much for a handgun. With a rifle he could have put down both Benito and Royce. He realized he was considering a cold-blooded kill and the realization surprised him. He could kill, and often had without too much provocation, but he was no out-and-out backshooter – even though he could have done it without effort in the case of Benito and Royce.

He had little time to reflect on the matter. The confrontation seemed to be over. The mounted Apaches turned their ponies away and cut off across the basin. As they cleared the stream they broke into pairs, riding in different directions. They would search the basin from end to end and they would not miss a trick. They would find his tracks. The place where he'd entered the basin. But they wouldn't find which way he'd gone after the explosion the previous night. The marks of his passing were long gone, wiped out by the trampling herd he had freed from the corral.

Last night he had almost given up hope of finding a place to hide. When at last he had reached the higher level of the cliff dwellings he prowled silently along the galleries, and with each passing minute his tension increased. Maybe he had been wrong walking into the heart of the Apache stronghold. Maybe he would have done better out in the basin, taking his chances in the rough terrain. Out there he might have found better cover, but he would have lessened his chances of getting close to Benito and Royce. He realized he was getting jumpy, seeing demons where none existed.

The uppermost gallery came to an end and he searched the shadows. There seemed nowhere to go now he had reached the upper levels. The only way now would be to go back down. But that was impossible. Benito's Apaches had stoked up the fires, driving the shadows from the area immediately in front of the cliff dwellings.

Brand pressed tight against the rock as a shadowed figure emerged from one of the houses. He watched the Apache woman descend to the lower level, and he knew he had to move. He couldn't stay where he was all night without being discovered. He moved to the extreme limit of the gallery, eyes searching the rock face above the houses. And spotted a place he could use. With both his guns tucked away Brand stepped up on to the wall that edged the gallery, using it to give him access to the roof of the end building. There was a ledge some six feet deep cutting back into the rock face. He hauled himself up and rolled into the deep shadow. Brand stretched out on his makeshift bed. It was not going to be comfortable, but he wasn't there for the fun of it.

From his position he had a clear view of the camp below. With daylight he would be able to see clear across the basin. Brand checked his weapons, laid one of the revolvers on the rock beside him, and after that he slept. . . .

Now the time for sleep was over. The camp below him was almost deserted, save for the women and children and few aged Apache warriors. Benito and Royce stood together talking. Royce's hired guns were scattered around the area. Brand wondered where Lucilla was. She wouldn't be far away. He made a mental note to keep an eye out for her. After last night she would be in a killing mood. He had no illusions where she was concerned. When he had been searching for her father she had not hesitated in hiring men to kill him – the next logical step would be to do the job herself, and Brand found it easy to visualize her doing it.

He stared out across the basin. Most of the Apaches were out of sight, having ridden to the far side. Brand knew this was going to be his best chance – maybe his only chance to get at Benito. He knew the risks but it was part of the job. Putting his life on the line had become as normal as pulling on a clean pair of socks. He did it without conscious thought. In truth it wasn't something he needed to spend too much time thinking about.

Brand swung himself over the ledge and dropped down to the gallery. He moved quickly, a Colt in each hand, his gaze alternating between Benito and Royce, and the distant Apaches.

He had reached the last but one level when a gaunt-faced Apache woman stepped out of a door just ahead of him. For long seconds she stared at him, her dark face blank of any expression. Beneath her tattered dress her body was thin. She looked half-starved. The frozen moment stretched, then Brand saw she was going to start yelling, and he wasn't close enough to stop her.

'*Pinda Lickoyi!*' the woman screamed and there was nothing frail about her voice. It soared up and out, bouncing off the rock face, echoing across the basin.

Bran swore violently. His moment of surprise had gone. Already the men down below were reacting, starting to move. Brand had little time left to regain any advantage.

He ran past the Apache woman, reaching the end of the gallery, turning to move on to the last slope that would take him to ground-level. A gun cracked spitefully, the bullet chewing splinters of rock from the gallery wall, spitting them into his face.

Brand twisted his upper body, eyes searching for the shooter, and saw one of Royce's gunhands. The gun in Brand's left hand came up and he triggered a quick shot at the man. The bullet kicked up dirt close to the man's boots and he took a step back, a fatal move. Instead of staying his ground and taking a second shot, he allowed precious seconds to slip away. Brand brought up his right-hand gun. This one was his own Colt, a weapon he knew as well as his own fingers. When he triggered two close shots he saw them both hit home, hammering into the target's chest. The shots slammed the man to the ground where he lay kicking away the last moments of his life, blood pumping from his chest.

Brand didn't stay to watch him fall. He knew he had hit the man and that was enough. He kept on moving. Bullets chipped at the rocks around him. One burned his left thigh, high up, and he felt warm blood start to flow. Brand caught sight of other figures running in his direction: the rest of Royce's hired guns. He kept on moving, letting them come to him.

As they neared him, leaving themselves in the open, Brand stopped in his tracks, both revolvers rising to the firing position. He faced the advancing men, the guns in his hands firing again and again, smoke wreathing around his motionless figure as he brought down the gunmen in a short, violent few heartbeats. They stumbled, fell, bodies torn and bloody from the barrage of shots. One struggled to return fire but Brand was already bringing his left-hand gun around for a final shot that caught the gunman just above the left eye. The heavy .45 bullet cored in through the skull and blew out the back of the man's head, jerking him off his knees, a red mist trailing after him as he crashed to the hard ground.

Benito and Royce had broken apart. Brand had glimpsed their move as he neared the end of the gallery. He didn't want to give them time to get too far. He did not want a dragged-out affair. Benito's Apaches would have heard the shooting and they would be on their way back, which gave Brand no damn time at all. As he trailed after Benito and Royce, Brand calmly reloaded his pair of Colts, one at a time, so that before he had to expose himself too much he had both weapons fully loaded.

He ignored the last steps, throwing himself forward, away from the protection of the gallery. The hard ground slammed against his left shoulder. Brand let his own weight carry him forward, rolling a couple of times as he picked up the sound of hard shots. Bullets furrowed the ground close by. Brand caught a blurred glimpse of Parker Royce, only yards away, saw the crazed gleam in the man's eyes. Royce was shooting without pause, making no deliberate attempt to place his shots. They went wild.

Brand's did not. He pushed out his right arm, held

for a second then fired, the bullet catching Royce in the face. He heard Royce's agonized scream and had a swift impression of the man falling, his hands cupped over his face: hands streaked with blood.

A gun fired. Something ripped through Brand's left arm, impacting against flesh. Brand lurched to his knees, turning his body in the direction of the shot, and saw Benito, his face bitter and hateful.

Benito – the renegade – the one who had tortured and maimed Nante. Brand recognized Benito, yet at the same time he saw a stranger. This Benito had a twisted mask for a face. Bitterness shone in Benito's dark-shadowed eyes. They were sunk deeply in his gaunt, lined face. The face of a madman who had gone far beyond reason. One who showed no mercy to others, whether they were white or Apache.

For a long moment the two faced each other. They both knew the outcome of this confrontation. There would only be one left to walk away.

Brand had no doubt in his mind who that would be – and he responded in the only way he knew.

His pair of Colts fired as one. He triggered two shots from each gun. Saw the stunning impact as the bullets tore into Benito's body, dropping him to the ground. Benito dropped the rifle he had been cocking and stayed on his hands and knees, head down, blood dripping from the open wounds in his chest. At last he raised his head, spitting blood from his lips as he stared across at Brand.

'It is not ended, Brand. You will not leave this place alive.' Benito spat into the dust again. 'Here you will die, *Pinda Lickoyi*!'

'Not by your hand, you bastard,' Brand said and raised his left-hand gun, placing the last four shots in its chamber into Benito's skull. The Apache lurched away from him, crashing to the ground in a heap, his shattered skull spewing bloody gore across the hard earth.

Brand dropped the empty Colt from his left hand, seeing blood dripping from his fingers. His arm was starting to go numb. As he stood upright he picked up the sound of hoofs on the ground. He ignored the sound as he replaced the spent cartridges in his own Colt. Only when he had finished did he look up.

A semicircle of mounted and armed Apaches stared back at him. Behind them were the women and children of the camp. Brand glanced at the line of stern faces. He recognized many of the Apaches from Nante's old band. There had been times in the past when he had spoken with them, shared food and drink. It didn't exactly make him a member of the Apache nation, but it gave him a slight edge – maybe enough of one to keep him alive.

'Benito is dead,' he said. 'The dying wish of Nante has been honored. Nante was put to the torture and another became leader in his place. Yet even though he lay dying Nante still thought as your leader. He saw that Benito would only· lead you to destruction. Make widows of your women and orphans of your children. He knew me as friend of the Apache, which is true, and asked me to free you from Benito.' Brand crossed to where Benito lay and rolled the body over with his foot. 'This one spoke of spirit protection. He told you he could not be harmed. He lied. Benito

140

had no spirits to aid him. He was driven only by hatred and this cowardly *Pinda Lickoyi*.'

Brand pointed to the curled-up figure of Parker Royce, motionless except for the pained shudders that racked his body.

Turning back to the silent Apache Brand asked:

'Where is Che?'

'I am here!'

The line of warriors parted to allow a rider to move into view. Brand watched the Apache as he slid from his pony to stand before him.

'Che, you know me. I do not lie to the Apache.' He watched for a change in the Apache's face and saw nothing, 'You were the one who found the trail of the one called Lobo for me. I made a promise I would seek him out and kill him. Did I keep that promise?'

Che's dark head moved slightly.

'The word is known that you killed the renegade.'

'You trusted me then, Che. And you trusted Nante's word also. Why did you turn on him like wolves when you should have heeded his counsel?'

The look in Che's eyes told Brand that the Apache was unsure of his ground at that moment.

'Benito promised us great things,' Che said abruptly. 'We are Apache. We are *The People*. Do we surrender like children who ask forgiveness? The *Pinda Lickoyi* has betrayed us too many times. Nante had grown old listening to their words and wanted a death in peace.'

'Nante died as wise as he had ever been,' Brand said. 'He wanted that peace for his people. He had seen that the Apache had to stop fighting the *Pinda*

Lickoyi before they were all destroyed. Before I left San Carlos I was visited by Geronimo. He spoke the words of Nante and will talk peace with Crook and Sieber. Che, I believe this time the peace will come. Even Cochise is beginning to think of talking for a surrender.'

'This is true?'

Brand nodded.

'Even the Apache can't fight for ever, Che. Look at your women and children. They grow weaker and thinner as each day passes. And it won't get better. Surrender doesn't bring shame down on a man, Che, because it takes a sight more courage to quit than it does to fight on. Each time you lose a warrior it gets harder to replace him. It isn't going to get better. Do you carry on the way you are? Hiding, running, moving camp until there are none of you left? This is not for the Apache. And not for the reason Benito wanted you to fight on.

'Benito was like Lobo. Full of hate that blinded him to the truth. Just like Benito's white friend. Che, I know this man. We are old enemies. When he gave you guns and whiskey and sent you to kill the *Pinda Lickoyi* it was not to help the Apache. It was for himself because he has a great hate for his own people. The woman too. Che, they have used the Apache for their own purposes.'

Che listened and considered Brand's words. Then he turned and walked back to talk with his people. Brand watched. He was sweating and it wasn't all from the heat.

He caught movement off to his left and saw

Lucilla. She went to where Royce lay and knelt beside him. She sat him up, pulling his hands from his bloody face. Brand heard her gasp of dismay. Brand's bullet had caught Royce in the left, lower jaw, tearing away most of the flesh and bone, leaving a raw, gaping wound. The spinning bullet had carried on to cleave Royce's cheek and eye. Royce looked a mess. He had already lost a great deal of blood and it was still pouring from the wounds. It was more than likely that the man would die out here on this lonely mountain.

Che returned to confront Brand.

'If it was left to some you would be dead,' Che said. 'But many know you as an honest man. They say you have always spoken the truth to the Apache. They want you to tell them what to do.'

'Get them on the trail back to San Carlos. Talk to Crook and Sieber. Make peace and live.'

Che stared at him for a moment, his impassive brown face betraying none of his thoughts. He was about to turn away when Lucilla's voice broke the silence.

'Don't listen to him. Benito is dead but you are still alive. Your hearts are still those of true Apaches. The whites *are* your enemies The Yankees who took your land are the ones who stole ours after the war. They must be killed. Destroy them and wipe them out.' Lucilla's voice rose to frantic shrillness. She jabbed a finger at Brand. 'He is a Yankee lawman. He is not to be trusted. He will lead you into a trap that will kill you all.'

As she uttered the final condemnation Lucilla

fumbled with the folds of her dress, pulling something into view. Something she thrust into Royce's
hand.

'*Now, Parker! Now!*' she screamed.

Brand saw Royce raise his arm, a revolver in his
hand. There was no hesitation in Brand's reaction.
He pushed Che aside, out of the line of fire and his
right hand brought up his Colt. The hammer was
already locked back as he levelled the weapon and
put two shots into Royce's body, seeing it jerk as the
heavy .45 caliber bullets punched bloody holes in
Royce's chest. Royce grunted under the impact. He
fell back against Lucilla. The revolver in his hand
went off, driving the bullet into the ground.

Brand held his weapon on Royce until he slipped
away from Lucilla, falling face down to the ground.

And then he saw the twin patches of red staining
Lucilla's dress just under the left breast. The patches
spread, merging into a single stain. Lucilla made a
soft sound, looking directly at Brand.

'Looks like you win after all, Mr Brand,' she whispered. She held his stare, blood running from the
corner of her mouth. She slumped forward, and
Brand barely caught her final words as she lay down.

'*Damn you to hell . . .*'

CHAPTER 14

Che sent one of the Apache women to tend Brand's wound. He sat in impassive silence as she cut out the bullet lodged just beneath the skin. She carried out the task with skill and speed, giving him no chance to protest. While she bandaged the arm Brand watched the gathered Apaches. He would have given an arm and a leg to be able to hear what they were saying. He was too far away to pick up what they were discussing. Judging by the raised arms and waving fists it appeared to be a heated argument. A lot depended on the outcome, not least Brand's own life. He was still alive by default. His fate had yet to be decided.

The Apache woman finished binding his arm. Brand thanked her. She studied him for a moment, then turned and walked away.

Brand leaned his back against the warm rock, hat pulled down over his eyes. From where he sat he could see the dark stain on the ground where the spilled blood from Royce and Lucilla still showed. The bodies had been taken away but the image remained in his mind. The look on Lucilla's face as she died. Still hating. Still ready to destroy. She had been a beautiful young woman and for that Brand was sorry she was dead. But she had involved herself in her father's, and then Royce's dirty affairs, right up to her neck. Where that was concerned he had no guilty feelings. Lucilla had dealt into a rough game. One that had no rules and did not recognize the difference between men and women when it came to dealing out losing hands.

Her father would have been proud of her, Brand decided. As far as he was concerned the whole damn family had been loco. Their wild schemes had caused widespread misery and suffering. As far as Brand was concerned the world was damn sight better off with them all out of the way.

None of it mattered a damn right now. None of it helped him in his current predicament.

He was alone, on the edge, and no amount of guessing was going to tell him the outcome. All he could do was hope he had talked fast enough to give the Apaches a basis to discuss their own problems.

He sat and waited. At noon they were still talking. Brand glanced up as a shadow moved nearby. It was one of the Apache women. She held out a bowl of food and a mug of what turned out to be a vicious brew of coffee. The bowl was half-full of a greasy stew that was heavily spiced but not so much that Brand didn't detect the taste of horsemeat. He was hungry enough not to give a damn. He had eaten horse before, but not often enough actually to become accustomed to it. He used his fingers to scoop up the stew, washing it down with the thick, gritty coffee.

146

Afterwards he felt around in his shirt pocket and found a crushed, part-smoked cigar. He still had a couple of matches left so he lit up and settled back.

And that was when he spotted three riders coming in along the trail that led into the basin from the cliff beyond. Two of the riders were Apache bucks. The third rider he recognized immediately.

It was Niana.

He stood up and watched them ride into camp. When they were near he walked out to meet them. Niana saw him and angled her pony towards him. The bucks cut off towards the corrals and Brand saw that one of them was leading *his* pony on a rope.

Niana slid from her pony. She ran her eyes over him, noting the fresh bruises, the torn and bloody shirt and the bandage around his left arm.

'I have brought your rifle,' she said, holding out the weapon for him to take.

Brand smiled wearily.

'I could have done with this a while back,' he told her.

Niana glanced around the camp.

'It is done?'

'It's done.'

'Benito? The *Pinda Lickoyi* who brought the guns? They are dead?'

He nodded.

'You have killed them all?'

'Yeah.'

Brand claimed credit for the deed, but there was no satisfaction. *How could there be?* How many had died since he had left San Carlos? He wouldn't let

147

himself figure out the total. It was done now. And it was over. He was content to let it rest.

'Last night I heard much noise. Shooting and a great explosion. Today more shooting.' She touched his arm. 'I disobeyed you, Brand. In my heart I could not forget you and thought you might be hurt. So I came to find you – but I was discovered and brought here.'

'Hell, it's nice to see a friendly face.'

'Apaches make talk. Hold council. Will they go to San Carlos?'

'It's what I'm waiting to hear. I made my case but I surely don't know if it did any good.'

Niana smiled. 'Do you still live?' she asked, and when he nodded she went on: 'Then you spoke well. If your words had not touched their hearts you would be dead already.'

Somehow *her* words failed to convince Brand completely. He took her to where he had been sitting. They squatted in the dust and Brand leaned his rifle close by. He squinted up at the sun-bright sky. It was going to be a long wait, he decided.

Mid-afternoon, and a figure detached from the distant group of Apaches and approached Brand.

It was Che.

'It is good to see the granddaughter back with her people, Niana,' the Apache said. 'I mourn that Nante is dead, but my heart gladdens at your sight.'

Niana smiled shyly, lowering her eyes.

'It pleases me to look upon you again, Che.'

Brand suddenly felt he was playing gooseberry. He climbed stiffly to his feet.

'*Che?*'

The Apache looked him in the eye, his own expression giving nothing away.

'We have talked. Now it is over. We have made our choice, Brand. We have reached a decision.'

CHAPTER 15

Al Sieber slammed his pen down in disgust and screwed up the report he'd been trying to write for the last hour. He flung the ball of paper aside and scrubbed a big hand across his face.

It was all a damn waste of time.

The days and weeks spent chasing all across the territory after Geronimo, all a damned waste. Geronimo would show himself when *he* decided it was the right time. Until then he would remain hidden for as long as he wanted, and not even Crook could flush him out. Not this time. Even Sieber and his scouts couldn't find the Apache. And Sieber was tired of trying. He wanted a rest. But he knew he wouldn't get one. Crook was back at Fort Apache for the moment. He would give his men a day or so of rest and then they would be off again.

'Shit,' Sieber muttered.

He got up from behind his desk and crossed to the stove. He picked up the coffee pot and poured himself a cup. He wandered towards the door, leaning his great bulk against the frame and stared out across San Carlos. The reservation stewed in the heat. Nothing was moving. It was too damned hot to move. The heat danced up off the hard earth, the glare hurting Sieber's eyes. He drank his coffee, gazing off into the far distance, seeing nothing.

'Hey, Al, we got callers.'

Sieber jerked out of his reverie. He saw Tom Horn standing there, a wide grin on his face.

'What you smirkin' at? All I was doin' was some thinking.'

Horn nodded. 'Sure, Al.'

'Visitors you say? Where?'

Tom Horn pointed out beyond the reservation. A pale cloud of dust rose against the blue sky. Ahead of the dust was a large group of riders, with others on foot, and they were making directly for San Carlos.

'Now who. . . ?' Sieber asked.

'Only one I can think of,' Horn said.

Sieber suddenly grinned. He tossed his empty cup on to the window sill and grabbed his hat off its peg.

'Damn me if he don't gone an' done it.'

He strode to the middle of the compound and stood, hands on hips, watching the approaching group come closer. He stayed where he was until they rode into San Carlos and drew to a halt.

'Hello, Al.'

Sieber glanced at the dusty, unshaven and gaunt-faced man who spoke to him from the back of an Apache pony. A tall, dark-haired man with bitter eyes, a grubby bandage around his left arm.

'Hell, you are a sorry sight, Jason.' Sieber waited until Brand dismounted. 'But it is damn good to see you. And your friends.'

Brand beckoned a young Apache forward.

'Che, this is Al Sieber. He's a good man. You can take his word as you take mine.'

Sieber nodded to the Apache.

'Che, let's get your people settled. I guess you all could use food and water.'

Brand turned away to let Sieber take over. This was his department. Brand had done his part.

'*Brand!*'

He turned at the sound of his name. It was Che. The Apache sat his pony, looking down at Brand. There was a moment of considered silence before Che spoke.

'Brand – it is well done?'

Jason Brand nodded. 'Yes, Che, it is well done.'

'*Enjuh*, Brand.'

Che nodded, satisfied. He raised his hand then turned his pony to where Sieber waited, and gave the people of Nante into the hands of the *Pinda Lickoyi*.

As Che left him Brand continued on into the admin building. All he wanted now was to get cleaned up and get some sleep. He almost missed the figure leaning against the wall near the door.

'Good trip?' Tom Horn asked, his tone pleasant enough.

Brand gazed at him with aching eyes. He noticed the shadow of a faint scar on Horn's jaw at just about the spot he'd hit the man. A thin smile edged his lips.

'All the better for seeing you, Tom,' he said quietly and walked on by.

He located the small room he had used last time and dumped his gear and rifle in a corner. He took off his gunbelt and hung it over the back of a chair close to the low cot he would sleep on. After a struggle he got his boots off. He took off his socks too, enjoying the coolness of the floor under his bare feet. Brand peeled off his shirt. That was when he remembered there were no washing facilities in the room. He debated for a moment. The lure of the cot was too much to resist. He decided to sleep first and get cleaned up later. He had only been stretched out for a couple of minutes before he heard a tap at the door.

'Yeah?'

'It is Niana.'

'Come on in.'

She stood looking down at him.

'I have come to say goodbye.'

'You leaving?'

'I am leaving the world I shared with you to return to my people.' Her dark eyes searched his face. 'You understand?'

'Guess so. And I'm real sorry.'

'We both go our own way. But I will always remember you, Jason Brand. My thoughts will be of you often.'

Brand stood up and she came to him. He held her for a time. There was no hesitation as she rose on her toes to kiss him. Her mouth was soft and moist. Brand felt the press of her firm breasts against his chest and for a moment he almost let himself weaken. Yet it was Niana who stepped back, face flushed, eyes searching his face. Then she smiled.

'May the spirits ride with you, *schichobe*,' she said, and then she turned and was gone.

EPILOGUE

Crook had his peace talks with Geronimo and the Apache agreed to surrender. But fate stepped in once again. The morning after the talks, Geronimo, who appeared to be drunk according to observers at the time, changed his mind and led his people away.

General Nelson A. Miles took over from Crook, and during the long months that followed he pursued Geronimo relentlessly. Aided by Tom Horn, who did a great deal to ease the way towards talks with the Chiricahua's leader, Miles eventually got Geronimo to surrender once more. This time the agreement held.

It was the beginning of the end of Apache resistance. By the end of the year Geronimo and his people had been transported to Fort Marion, Florida. Later they were sent to Mount Vernon Barracks on the Mobile River in Alabama. The place was a breeding ground for sickness, and after much pleading by people like George Crook and John

Clum, Geronimo and his people were sent to Fort Sill, Oklahoma in 1894. There they were to remain. Geronimo died in 1909 and was buried in the Apache cemetery. It is said that his bones were eventually removed and returned to his native South-west. Back to the land he had fought so long to keep for his Apaches.

Despite his success with the Army Tom Horn eventually moved on. He became a Pinkerton Detective and stayed with them until the early 1890s. At this time his life took a complete change. Moving to Cheyenne Horn hired out as a Range Detective to a number of unnamed cattle barons. Range wars and trouble with nesters and sheepmen meant there was ample work for a hired gun – which was actually what Horn had become. He killed a fair number of men during his employment and built a reputation as being cold-blooded in the execution of his trade. In 1902 the cattle men were still at war with the sheep-herders. It was in that year that Tom Horn made his final kill and ultimately his first mistake when he shot and ambushed a fourteen-year-old boy. The shooting was fatal. There were various reports about the killing. It was generally accepted that Horn had shot the boy by mistake – he had been lying in wait for the child's father. A US deputy marshal managed to become friendly with Horn – to the extent of getting him drunk enough to admit killing the boy. To ensure that the confession was not wasted, the deputy – a man named Joe LeFors – had witnesses hiding nearby and word-for-word notes were taken. Tom Horn was subsequently arrested and stood trial. The jury found him guilty and Horn was sentenced to hang. Though many thought he would escape paying the price Tom Horn had no way out this time. In November of 1903 he climbed the steps of the gallows, and was hanged with a rope he had made while sitting in his cell. It was a bitter end to a career that had started out so well.

If his father had not been murdered by another Indian, the Apache Kid's life might have turned out differently. Al Sieber explained to the Kid the need to bring the killer in to stand trial. But the Kid was still an Apache and he obeyed tribal law, tracking down the murderer and executing him. Afterwards the Kid and his companions rode into San Carlos to surrender to Sieber. Sometime during the parley an Apache started shooting. In the ensuing mêlée that followed the gunshots the Apache Kid and his companions made their escape. Al Sieber sustained a wound in one foot – a wound that became one of the factors in his eventual departure as Chief of Scouts.

The Apache Kid fled San Carlos, taking the trail he was to follow for the rest of his life. Though the big names of the Apache nation faded from the public memory in the near future the Apache Kid was to remain a talking point for many years. Years during which he engaged in a single-handed war against the white population of the South-west, and mainly directed at the US Army.

The battle lasted until 1894. Then the lone Apache Kid vanished. A man named Edward Clark, a former scout himself, whose partner the Kid had killed five years before, was camping at Rifle Springs. He fired on two Apaches, a man and a woman, who tried to steal his horses. The woman died. The man escaped. Clark was certain it had been the Apache Kid and insisted he had wounded him. No body was ever found and Edward Clark went to his grave still claiming it had been the elusive renegade and that his, Clark's, bullet had ended the Apache Kid's life.

All that was certain was that the Apache Kid had disappeared.

Speculation was rife for years to come. Had the Kid been hit by Clark? If it genuinely had been the Apache Kid, had he managed to crawl away to die in some lonely place? Or had he made it across the border into Sonora and lost himself in his Sierra Madre hideout? There were many theories and they all remained unanswered. The only answer to them all was – *quien sabe?*

Who knows?

The mystery remained and persisted. If anyone knew the truth they stayed silent, perhaps realizing there was no point in adding to the speculation surrounding the Apache Kid's disappearance. Then again there were those who kept their own counsel, seeing no gain in spreading their own glory. If they achieved something, the doing of the deed was enough in itself.

The Apache Kid rose from sergeant in Al Sieber's scouts to became a legend, and legends have a way of lingering long after the fact has ceased to provide answers.

*

After a few days rest ex-US Marshal Jason Brand saddled up and rode out of San Carlos. He never returned to the reservation. He did meet up with Al Sieber a number of times, but only heard the stories about Tom Horn – which suited him. Once clear of San Carlos he put his horse on the trail that led down into Mexico. There was a small ranch there and he had promised Sarita that he would return. For once he wanted to keep a promise.

Somewhere at the back of his mind he had the feeling his time with her was limited. News of his involvement with Crook and Sieber would eventually reach Washington and once that happened it would filter through to Frank McCord – that was if McCord had not already found out where Brand had been taking his unofficial break. It would not be a surprise to find someone waiting for him at Sarita's.

One way or another McCord would summon him, and Brand knew he would respond. The St Clair affair had been settled once and for all, and that settling had finalized his grieving over Sarah Debenham's death.

Brand knew now there was no escaping his destiny. It wasn't as if he had any other choice. What else was there for a man such as himself? Where was there he could go to escape? And if he did elude that destiny what would he find to replace it?

Jason Brand had the answers even as he formed the questions in his mind.